Luna

Thank you for
your support and
for being a wonderful
presence in this
world and
in my life

Carmen

Luna

CASSANDRA SHOFAR

Contents

Acknowledgements

I am eternally grateful to all who supported me, inspired me and helped me create the world of Luna Fortella, whose story carried me through the many intense peaks and desolate valleys of a true "Dark Night of the Soul." I thank my parents and family for always believing in me, no matter what. I thank my friends and loved ones for being the most amazing "Spirit Tribe" I could ever ask for. And I thank all of the wonderful, strong, intelligent, beautiful, passionate, inspiring and empowering women in my life and in the world. Never be afraid of your own magic. Never be afraid to shine.

For Diane

Prologue

The aged stonewalls were dewy with last night's rain, the dank scent of mold seeping from the dark corners of the room. But the rest of the dilapidated enclosure blazed red from the fire outside the barred windows. She shuddered, her bones suddenly icy with fear.

The ropes around her wrists cut into her damp skin, causing her to wince and grit her teeth. The pebbles growled beneath her as she dragged her bare, cut and calloused feet under her legs, hugging her dirt-caked knees to her chest.

Hearing the scuffle, the guard turned his surly face and pursed lips her way, revealing severe, yet placid eyes that seemed to look straight through her. Whatever spell she was accused of having on others did not seem to stretch its gnarled claws his way.

She sniffled and he turned away, looking at the entrance once more, her presence nothing but an afterthought. Slowly, she began rocking back and forth, the rhythmical movement providing a tangent of solace. Though the barbed tentacles of terror pierced her parched throat, somehow her vocal cords found vibration. She began to hum a soft, low melody her mother used to sing to her as a child upon waking from the dark grasp of a nightmare. Its rich, mournful notes, laced with sharps and flats, brought chills down the guard's spine, though his expression remained blank.

Chains, crimson with rust, sliced into her ankles and clanked against the cold, muggy floor. She could hear both screams and cheers outside the sole window of her cell, as though a riot were brewing. Each crackle of the fire, as logs collapsed beneath its scalding flames, seemed to puncture her skin.

Suddenly, the creaking strain of a door slashed through her dismal song, jarring her attention to the entrance of her cell. She heard footsteps approaching and felt the familiar tingling of his energy filtering through the bars and into her body, causing her heart to jump and her breath to violently catch.

Slowly, with precision and stifling pain, she stood, gripping the bars to provide balance as the tattered remains of a once vibrant peasant skirt shook around her legs. Her chestnut hair fell loosely down her back and shoulders. Its dark, wavy, auburn tendrils playfully tickled the hairs upon her arms and framed her mystic eyes, now fiery embers of emotion.

And just like that, he was there.

The older-looking guard escorting him stepped back, allowing a moment of privacy not required.

He stood before her – his solemn eyes locked onto hers, before briefly leaving their hold to gently skim over her shoulders, collarbones and delicate neck. A place his swollen lips had traced not but days earlier, now tarnished with dry blood from the ropes that had dragged her from the warm haven of their bed to this perdition.

He swallowed hard, his Adam's apple softly rising and falling under her steady gaze. His body shuddered from a sudden jolt of electricity as her eyes met his, now glistening with anger from the damage done to her – this beautiful creature he had given up everything for.

Her glowing irises mirrored his, emanating anguish over the bruises soiling his angelic forehead, shoulders and cracked ribs, all places her clement skin had grazed fervidly not long ago. All places she had memorized down to each exquisite freckle and scar.

Before another breath was expelled, he stepped a shackled leg forward and brought his tied hands to the sole bar in front of them, grasping her trembling fingers and closing all space between them.

His lips hungrily dove into hers, eagerly swimming in her energy. She softly parted them with her tongue, intertwining it with his. A fierce and familiar heat ignited both their hearts. The fiery glow that seemed worlds away whipped through the window and lit the tear streaming down his right cheek before glinting off the ones searing across both of hers.

The older guard cleared his throat, bursting their bubble and jolting them both from the trance.

"It is time," the man simply said, stepping forward and grasping her lover's right upper arm.

Nothing could be done. They both knew it.

"I love you," he whispered violently, his body pulled back by both guards, shattering his grip from her hands, her pulse.

"I love you, too," she managed through cracked vocal cords.

And just like that, he was gone.

A tremulous breath rippled through her, buckling her knees and sending her cascading to the floor, crippled by the excruciating agony planted in the depths of her core. Waves of sorrow rolled through her, tossing her body into billows of misery she could no longer control.

The crowd grew more boisterous, which could only mean his presence was made known amongst them.

A sharp click of the cell door pulled her from her bout with despondency, sending her head jerking toward the guard entering what little space she had left, like poison pervading a vein.

He bent down to pick her up, but her eyes shot up to his, stopping him in his tracks.

He backed up slightly, his face no longer a blank slate, but filled with apprehension and uncertainty.

Lethargically, she made her way to her tender feet, rattling the chains around her ankles. But her sound calf muscles fluidly contracted, sending her body forward. The guard followed suit, not daring to touch her flaming skin.

She exited the cell and walked down the short, decrepit hallway, past two more empty cells on her right. Then the giant, heavy oak prison door swung open, pouring smoke-filled dusk air into her lungs and causing the crowd to burst into more cries and shouts.

She paused and exhaled, shaking her mane of chocolate locks out of her face and wiping her eyes with her bound wrists.

She took a soft, graceful step forward.

The cluster of onlookers divided, making a path to the wooden steps 20 feet ahead. Some eyes cast to the dusty ground in fear, others looked at her dead on – hate in their charcoal pupils – while others gave fleeting glances of sadness and compassion.

Words of hate were spit at her, along with prayers spiraling at her feet.

But she paid no attention to any of this. She was looking for one pair of eyes, and only one.

She found them.

Surrounded by four armed guards, he stood, his oceanic, helpless irises fastened to hers. As she floated up the steps, it was as though the crowd suddenly vanished. Neither of them heard anything, only the potent heartbeat of the other.

The guard behind her untied her wrists, tersely pulling her arms backward to bind them around the wooden pole pressed firmly against her spine. Her teeth clenched in pain, but her eyes remained locked on his, her lips slightly parted and still swollen from his kiss.

Heat from the flames around her grazed her skin and hair, setting her dark eyes ablaze. Gasps were heard from onlookers brave enough to gander. The very priest who condemned her – who had said he, too, had succumbed to her spell, allowing its essence to fill his mind with unholy thoughts – stood cold and dark at the bottom of the steps.

"Any last words?" He asked, guilt like venom dripping from his mouth.

Yet her gaze never wavered. She kept her eyes on the stormy spheres of her mirrored soul as the world around her dispersed into the flames.

Everything went black.

Chapter 1

Luna stared at the bed knobs, focusing hard on the hand-carved wooden spheres choked off at the bottom by intricately woven Celtic knots. She'd never paid close attention to them before, though they had been her father's bed knobs since she could remember. Homing in on anything besides his nearly lifeless form under those threadbare, brown blankets would suffice at the moment.

Out of the corner of her eye, Luna saw his weak figure stir slightly, pulling her attention back to the very place she both loved and dreaded – his eyes. They were barely open, now an unfocused pale, cloudy blue. His thin lips parted as his gravelly voice came out in a whisper.

"Luna ... it is almost time," he rasped through weakened windpipes.

Her ash-colored eyes darkened with onyx swirls, instantly creating an emotional wall for what was to come. Her voice came out low and raspy, barely audible.

"Father, this is not your time. I cannot do this without you," she said slowly, controlling her emotions, though they were brooding beneath her surface. He gathered what strength he had left to respond.

"I have told you. Katrin has been able to find work for you in the king's estate. You must take it to help keep the manor going," he said, breaking into a wheezy fit of coughs. The sound toppled her wall, exposing vulnerability only he could. Her eyes suddenly lightened to a silvery gray and her creased brow softened.

"No Papa. That is not what I mean. I mean I cannot do life without you. Your wisdom, your protection."

At the latter, her father's eyes narrowed with understanding and fear.

"Since Mama was ... since she died, you have been my only

guidance," Luna added, shaking her head and burying her face in her hands. She felt her father lethargically move. His hand came up to the side of her head, clasping her long, dark locks as he used his thumb to wipe her tears.

"My Luna. You are a strong woman. You are your mother's daughter and a survivor. You will be okay. You have a strong group of workers here who have practically raised you for the last 10 years and love you as their own. And −" he paused, gauging her intent eyes, hanging on his every word. "You do not need to be scared. You just have to remember the things I told you about people, about society. Times are distressing, but you mustn't let that dictate your every breath. Just remain strong, true and steadfast. You will do just fine."

Luna breathed out and sniffled as her hand came up to cover her father's shaky fingers, pressing them harder against her face. Her heart splintered, squelching her next breath. It felt as though her body was enflamed. The familiar tingling burned under her father's cold, cradling touch.

He recognized the heat and immediately began shushing her the way her mother did when she turned feverish as a child. Instantly, her racing heart slowed and her skin cooled. He looked at her hard, a subtle warning behind his tired eyes and she quietly nodded. Her eyelids squeezed shut as she focused on her meticulous breathing; anything to pretend the one thing nobody could control had halted. But the steady sound of sand softly streaming through the hourglass on their mantel reminded her magic of that kind did not exist.

Luna felt her father's hand begin to go lax. She kept her eyes tightly shut and began rocking back and forth as she heard his breathing slacken.

"I love you, my Luna."

*****

Her eyes peeled open. She looked at the placid eyes of her father and felt his cold hand, now rigid. She wondered how long she had been sitting there. Looking over at the hourglass, Luna saw the bottom completely filled and realized she must have lost consciousness. Gently putting her father's arm down by his side and closing his eyelids, Luna methodically pulled the blankets all the way up to his chin and blew out the candle next to his head.

"Goodnight Papa."

Not bearing to look back at his listless form, Luna exited the room quietly, shutting the door behind her. Rounding the corner, Dirdra, her family's longtime servant, paused at the bottom of the steps with a basket of clothes in one arm, a candle in the other. She looked at Luna's vacant, ebony eyes and lowered the basket to the bottom step, quickly placing the candle on the flat end of the banister and pulling Luna's feeble body into a tight, warm embrace.

Perhaps it was the familiar scent of cranberries and lilacs or the circular rub of Dirdra's calloused hand on her back, or maybe it was just the relief of leaning onto another, but Luna broke into convulsing sobs. They seemed to burrow deep down, scraping out her insides before rising to the surface and leaving her hollow. Something dormant, buried inside her shifted.

"Oh, dear Jevan ... may he rest in peace," a tearful Dirdra whispered, squeezing Luna tighter.

After what seemed an eternity, Luna pulled back to find Dirdra's hand prepared with a handkerchief. She wiped her face and Dirdra nodded to their other servant, Regan, who had crept out from the kitchen. Both knew Luna would not be able to help prepare the body for the funeral, so Regan left to make the proper arrangements. Dirdra helped Luna's wary body upstairs to her room, eased her into her nightgown and tucked her into bed – the way she had for most of Luna's life.

She blew out the candle on the nightstand, shut the door behind her and left Luna to rest. Luna had barely slept in days, only nodding off here and there. Though slow at first, exhaustion – physical, mental and emotional – crept up and finally wrapped Luna in its suffocating grasp. She felt barren and the insistent tug of sleep pulled on her eyelids until she gave in, shutting out the world and relieving her sallow heart ... at least for the time being. She prayed that maybe she, like her father, would never have to open her eyes again.

Chapter 2

Three months passed in a cursory blur. The tender touch of Luna's father's hand dissipated with every moment lost to time's infinite appetite. In its place, a strange energy stirred, filling Luna's heart with morose uncertainty.

Since he had no son, Jevan left their manor and property to Luna's cousin, Melvan, who agreed to her father's wishes to allow Luna to run the manor in Melvan's absence – he had his hands full with five children and a farm to tend to three villages away.

The peculiar presence of something brewing inside Luna remained in the background of her mind as she prepared to meet Katrin at the market. Luna had only been working with Katrin a week, yet she felt as though she'd been running errands for the royal court for years. Yes, the linens were far more lustrous and extravagant, but alas, they were still linens that needed washing, just as the bedchambers, like any others, were in need of scouring and sweeping.

Between working half a day with Katrin and the rest of her time running their humble manor, Luna felt as though she were a candle being burned at both ends. And bless Regan – not but five years behind Luna – at 19, she was still such a dreamer. Every day, she asked Luna if she finally met a member of the court, or perhaps even saw the king himself. And every day, Luna would explain they purposely did their work in the shadows, often during times the royal family was away on business or the women were taking the air. Once, Luna caught a glimpse of Duke Nicolai, the king's most trusted confidant, but it was merely in passing and Luna cast her eyes immediately to the floor.

Using the ebony lace scarf her mother wore when mourning her own father, Luna wove the fabric through her raven locks, pulling them back in a makeshift braid. Her long black skirt and bodice made her porcelain skin look almost ashen save for the deep, cool plum color of her lips.

Dirdra was in the kitchen baking bread, its sweet yeasty aroma wafting up the stairs and greeting Luna as she made her way to the door.

"I am off to the market to meet Katrin," she said, hearing Dirdra's mumbled response as she shut the door behind her. Luna shook her head, meekly smiling. Sweet Dirdra, always in her own world when working.

The walk to the market was not too tiresome, only a few miles and a couple of turns. Luna inhaled the air, smelling the dewy grass and nectar-filled flowers. As she passed neighbors, Luna's eyes found the dirt road, always giving a slight bow, but rarely ever making eye contact. Some people audibly greeted her, often with tight, polite smiles. While others, seeing her mourning wear, gave their condolences. Luna was always amiable in turn, but cautious by nature, her father's words forever ingrained in her memory.

The familiar smells and sounds of the market met Luna as she turned the corner. Her body tensed up as her aversion to crowds settled in on her nerves, but she quickly spotted Katrin's broad shoulders and thick, wily brown hair peeking out from her headscarf. Almost simultaneously, Katrin looked up at her.

"Luna, there you are," she said hurriedly, making her way to Luna with a basketful of squash, potatoes and green beans.

"What is wrong?" Luna asked, seeing the stress lines on Katrin's brow.

"Duke Nicolai is visiting again today, but this time, with his sons. We have to prepare three bedchambers for them," she said. "I promised Mirium I would pick up some things at the market, but we must hurry back as they are to arrive in less than three hours."

Luna grabbed the basket from Katrin's hands as she pulled out her coin purse to pay for the produce. Then, they made their way to a one-horse buggy. Katrin let out a soft groan as she bent her arthritic knees to make room for Luna, who effortlessly hopped in.

They arrived at the castle's rear entrance 20 minutes later and walked through the kitchen to hand Mirium the basket of food. She quickly wiped her hands on her apron and hastily grabbed it from Katrin, thanking her twice over before returning to chopping onions.

Katrin led the way through the rear kitchen entrance and into the servants' corridor.

"Let's grab the linens now and we will take care of the beds first," she said, limping slightly as she maneuvered her bulky frame through the narrow doorway and into the vast room brimming with towels, sheets, pillowcases and curtains.

Finally, they arrived at the threshold of the first bedroom in the east wing of the castle, quickly working as a team to set the bed, polish the wood and open the drapes to let in the early afternoon sunlight. When the third room was complete, they sat down on the steps leading back down to the linens room to let Katrin catch her breath.

"Last minute guests are so vexing these days," she said, wheezing slightly. Luna asked if she needed her to go get water or a damp towel for her forehead, but Katrin tersely shook her head no. With Luna's help, as well as the railing, Katrin slowly rose to her feet.

The duke's arrival was announced shortly after, courtesy of an errand boy, as Luna and Katrin hastily helped Mirium in the kitchen.

Suddenly, Luna's hand shot up to the back of her hair. Feeling it loose and falling around her shoulders, she realized her scarf had somehow come undone.

My mother's scarf.

Panic flooded her veins as Luna searched the floor but saw nothing. Katrin said she did not recall seeing it anywhere either.

Knowing she was risking a sound lecture from Katrin if she returned to the guest bedchambers, Luna quickly excused herself to "step outside for air" and whisked up the servant stairway. When she reached the top, she paused, listening for any presence. Hearing nothing but the wind whistling through the corridor below and her own quickened breath, she tiptoed into the first room, quickly scanning the floor.

Nothing.

She moved to the next room, skimming the bed, floor, even the vanity. Alas, nothing. Beginning to panic more, Luna quietly exited the room and crept to the third room. Her heart racing, she pushed the door open, not noticing it was already slightly ajar.

Her eyes were immediately glued to the floor, unaware of the presence in the room until it was too late. She heard an audible creak in the floorboard ahead of her and slightly jumped.

"Oh," she exclaimed in shock, seeing a man who appeared a few years her senior standing at the foot of the opulent bed. He mirrored her slightly open-mouthed expression.

His features were refined, sharpened by the flicker of candlelight, but it was his piercing blue eyes that caught her attention. He had clearly begun disrobing, though it appeared he had not gotten far. Luna felt the familiar tingle in her skin as it began to flare, her eyes abashedly snapped to the floor.

"I, I am so very sorry, Your Grace," she stammered, slightly bowing forward and promptly backing up toward the door.

"Was it this you were looking for?" he asked, extending a hand holding her mother's scarf.

Mortified, she raised her eyes to his penetrating, yet amused gaze and quickly nodded, stepping forward to retrieve the scarf. His fingers lightly grazed hers, sending more tingles up her arm. She abruptly withdrew her hand. Clasping the scarf to her chest, she once again backed up toward the door.

"I did not mean to intrude, Your Grace. I thought the rooms were still unoccupied," she said, her voice low and strong as she finally regained her composure back, trying to reach inside for her usual indifference to the wealthy.

"It is alright," he said awkwardly, increasing the flush in Luna's skin as she realized he likely has never engaged with a young female servant in so intimate a setting as his bedchambers.

"Thank you Your Grace," she said, meeting his eyes once more before politely bowing and exiting the room.

She exhaled deeply and scurried down the hall, through the servant door and down the steps without a sound.

She never heard his door open again, or saw him stepping into the hallway, finding nothing but darkness in her wake.

Chapter 3

A month had passed, bidding spring adieu and embracing a squelching summer. Luna was helping Dirdra prepare dinner when she heard a curt knock on the door. Regan was there before Luna had even set her knife down. After a minute, Regan appeared in the kitchen doorway.

"It is Katrin. She wants to speak with you."

Luna untied and removed her apron, smoothed down her hair and skirts, and opened the door to a smiling, yet wearied Katrin. Her sage eyes always told more than she intended, a trait Luna shared as well.

"Katrin, how are you? Come in," Luna said, motioning to the sitting room on the right. Katrin stepped passed the threshold, the smell of raw onions, spices and parsley filling her nostrils.

"Mmmm, smells wonderful," she said, more to herself than Luna, as they walked into the parlor.

Regan had already started a pot of tea, quickly following behind them with cups and saucers, as well as bread, cheese and Dirdra's latest batch of pastries.

"Thank you Regan," Katrin said distractedly, organizing her thoughts and jumping right to the point.

"Luna, it would seem the king is planning to have several members of the court stay with him for a few months while they negotiate treaties with the south. We are going to need all the help we can get," she said, peering around the room slowly. Luna followed her gaze.

"What is it?" Luna asked.

"Well, I came to ask if you could possibly stay with us full-on for the next couple months and if Dirdra and Regan would be able to run things here for a bit," Katrin replied.

Luna sat quietly for a moment, pondering the proposition carefully. Dirdra had been running most of the manor since Luna's father died, though Luna helped where she could while earning enough wages working with Katrin to keep things going. Her cousin, Melvan, stopped by occasionally to check in, but he barely made enough wages to fill the mouths of his own family. This extra work would benefit them all financially, however, Luna was afraid to place too much strain on Regan and Dirdra.

They were a family now more than ever, and even with the part-time help they have with their livestock, Luna felt she had to consult with Dirdra before making this decision. She called her into the room and had Katrin repeat the proposal. After some deliberation, Dirdra looked at Luna.

"I think you should do it. It's only a few months, and we can pull our own here with the extra help we get from Kornel," she said, nodding toward their neighbor's house.

Luna looked at Dirdra hard, searching her hazel eyes for reservations, but there were none.

She nodded briefly and turned her eyes to Katrin.

"Okay."

Katrin sighed in relief. Gulping down the rest of her tea, she thanked all three of them before grunting in pain as she rose to her feet. Seeing her off, Luna stood in the doorway, leaning the side of her head against the frame and releasing a long, deliberate breath.

Something within her shifted again, perhaps foreshadowing more change.

*****

Having brought the last of her belongings to the estate, Luna felt the permanence of the next few months set in. She would only have a few days here or there to visit Dirdra and Regan, and the thought nimbly squeezed her heart.

Katrin and Luna already prepared all the guestrooms, each party arriving in intervals throughout the last week and a half.

"How many sons does Duke Nicolai have?" Luna asked nonchalantly, as she and Katrin filled buckets with water from the nearby well.

"Two. His Graces Caedon and Darius," she said quickly, glancing up at Luna before beginning to pull up the third bucket. Taking Luna's silence as a desire for more information, Katrin continued.

"Caedon is the eldest, at 30. and Darius is 24," she said. "Their mother died when they were but lads, and the duke never remarried."

Luna nodded at this but said nothing. Telling Katrin she had run into one of them – though she is sure now it must have been Caedon – would reveal she disobeyed servant rules that day, so instead, she filled a fourth bucket and they headed back to the kitchen in silence. While Katrin was perceptive and blunt when times called for it, she was more often refreshingly unobtrusive, much like Luna herself.

It still felt strange being at the king's castle after darkness fell, but Luna always had plenty to keep her occupied. She often retreated to the servants' quarters with a book and candle in hand to enjoy what little downtime she had.

Tonight felt strangely aberrant as Luna disrobed for the night and slid into her simple, off-white nightgown. She had sewn cloth ties on the back and fastened them quickly before sliding open her room's only window to let in the cool night air.

Suddenly, she heard voices outside. They seemed to be carrying over from the king's stables. Curiosity overtook Luna's usual respect for privacy as she leaned out the window, straining to make out the words.

"Father. I know what my responsibilities are. You remind me every day of my life," a man's voice said. Luna recognized it as the man she'd encountered before.

"Then why do you insist on putting this off any further?" the duke said, exasperated.

"Because I am not ready yet."

"You are 30 Caedon. I was 28 when I courted your mother. The duchess is 18 and the timing is right."

Luna heard nothing then, just the steady thrum of crickets. She ducked back into the room, feeling ashamed for eavesdropping as long as she had. She slid into her bed, pulled the cotton sheets up to her waist and blew out her candle.

*****

Luna was startled awake by the sound of whimpering. Investigating the sound, she found herself face to face with a large dog, some kind of Great Dane mix, in the hallway. Perplexed, Luna furrowed her brow and looked down the dark empty corridor, dimly lit by a few candles in wall sconces.

Recognizing the dog was friendly and eager to find its owner, Luna grabbed his collar and began walking toward the door leading to the foyer, where she hoped to find help. She saw the door was cracked, indicating the dog's point of entry. She gently pushed it open and saw Virgil, another servant, standing by the front entrance of the foyer.

"Virgil," she whispered, catching his attention. He looked from her to the dog and quickly made the connection.

"Oh, I see. Let me take him. I'm very sorry, Luna. How on earth did he get in?"

Luna pointed to the partially opened servants' door and he nodded in comprehension.

"It's you," a voice from the opposite end of the room said. Luna snapped her head to the right to see Caedon standing by a large marble column, a look of shock on his face. Luna could think of nothing else to say, so she just nodded and turned toward the servants' door.

"I guess we're even now," he said briskly, his tone weary.

Luna turned back toward him, puzzled by his meaning. Then she saw him motion toward the dog and realized it was his. Luna found it strange for a man of his station to have a mixed breed.

She suddenly became aware of the fact she wore nothing but a thin nightgown and had sleep-disheveled hair. Her eyes narrowed and lips pressed harder together as she realized Caedon also noticed.

Sensing her embarrassment, as well as his own, he swiftly thanked her and cast his eyes to the floor.

When he looked up a breath later, she was gone.

Chapter 4

Luna woke up with a stiff back and foggy thoughts. She rubbed her eyes and lightly shook her head. It took her a few minutes to realize the night before had not been a dream, strange as it was. She pulled her achy body out of bed and decided a hot bath would be the cure.

Once soaking in the tub, Luna closed her eyes and tried to clear her mind. It was Sunday, and though the servants did not attend church with the higher stations, they did visit the nearby chapel. Katrin would be waiting for Luna, so she briskly finished bathing and put on her usual black, layered skirt and bodice, lacing it up extra tight before pulling her hair back with her mother's scarf.

Sure enough, Katrin was in the hallway near the door leading out to the carriage, her eyes brightening when she saw Luna.

"Are you ready?"

Luna nodded and they stepped outside into a drizzling rain, casting a silver sheen on the building's stone walls and walkway. When they arrived at the chapel, they quickly made their way to the front entrance, a rumbling thunder chasing them through the whitewashed doors.

Luna tensed up. She still had not gotten used to the new parish. In fact, she had never been comfortable in the church, but at least the parish near her manor was familiar.

Suddenly, her father's milky blue eyes flashed in her mind, warning her. She let out a gradual breath through her softly parted lips and slid into the very last pew with Katrin, their combined weight causing the wood to creak and a few people to stir.

The priest read a few passages, while Luna made sure to keep her eyes low. When the service completed, everyone filed toward the doors, but Katrin, as usual, preferred to wait until the chapel cleared out before moving. Using the back of the pew in front of them, she pushed herself up, her knees audibly cracking, drawing a wince.

Luna made her way to the end of the pew when she suddenly felt her skirt being tugged, caught on a nail. As she worked the fabric gently, she saw Katrin had already walked through the chapel doors.

"Here, let me help you," a voice said. Luna looked up to see the middle-aged priest reach forward to help her unhook the cloth. Her silvery eyes met his and he seemed to pause, transfixed. She heard his breathing change, becoming slightly more rapid as he stepped back, realizing he was only inches from her.

"Thank you," she said promptly, looking down and swishing past him toward the doors.

Once outside, Luna felt immediately at ease, her shoulders and neckline softened as she closed her eyes and turned toward the sky. The raindrops had grown more potent since the morning, causing her eyelids to flinch as they landed on her cheeks and forehead. But the water practically sizzled as it cooled her flushed skin.

"Luna, come now ... you'll catch a cold," Katrin shouted from the carriage, startling Luna from her trance.

She scuttled down the steps, unaware of the priest's eyes staring through the stained glass window — and even more oblivious to the sapphire eyes of the duke's son, sitting on a horse in the road, strangely caught by the scene.

*****

Four days passed, as the ominous skies and relentless showers enjoyed overstaying their welcome. Luna and Katrin worked eagerly to finish washing the last load of sheets for the day. Lost in the steady vibration of the washing board beneath her raw fingers, Luna closed her eyes and began humming a low melody. They were notes Dirdra often sang when she worked, and Luna allowed them to temporarily whisk her away from the castle and into the kitchen at the manor. She imagined Dirdra baking fresh rolls, their sweet, buttery smell assailing her senses.

"Luna," Katrin said softly, pulling her back to the tedious work at hand. Katrin motioned for her to hand over the sopping sheet to hang up. She did so and asked whether she could be excused to her room to rest. Katrin, who had planned to do the same, agreed to an hour break for lunch.

Instead of retreating to her room, however, Luna decided to get some air, even though it was still sprinkling outside. She pulled a shawl out of the chest in her room and wrapped it around her head. Without a single thought, she headed toward the king's stables, feeling a peculiar urge to see the stallions and mares. She looked around to check for others before slipping inside.

The sweet smell of fresh hay and rich soil greeted her, but it was the shuffling hooves and soft nickering from the barn that made Luna's lips curl into a smile. She walked up to the painted mare in the corner. She neighed quietly and moved toward Luna's outstretched hand, gently nudging her palm.

Luna vaguely heard the sound of a woman talking outside the stables, followed by the low rumble of a man's voice. She sucked in her breath and held it, praying they weren't coming inside.

But her plea went unanswered. The voices grew louder and Luna had nowhere to turn as the rear doors to the barn were locked.

"Thank you, Your Grace," the woman said. She sounded quite young, Luna thought distractedly, trying to home in on the man's response.

"You're welcome," he said curtly, his voice ringing in Luna's ears. She instantly placed it as Caedon's.

"I was hoping to see your horse," the woman said timidly. Luna assumed this was the duchess Duke Nicolai was speaking of the other night.

Caedon cleared his throat and stepped toward the barn door, beginning to open it. Luna, realizing she was still holding her breath, released it and began frantically searching for a place to hide. Unfortunately, she missed her step and fell to the dirt floor, banging against a bucket and letting out a short, high-pitched gasp.

The barn door stopped opening. Save for the horses stirring at the minor ruckus, it was completely silent. Luna once again held her breath, feeling her heart racing, her skin tightening with heat.

"How about I show him to you tomorrow, Duchess Rosalind?" he asked, rather abruptly.

She must have nodded in agreement for Luna heard them withdraw from the barn, their voices slowly dwindling.

Sluggishly, Luna got up, dusted herself off, gave the mare she had been admiring a quick pat and then slipped out of the barn. As she scrambled to get to the servants' wing, she felt eyes on her, causing her to halt and look to her right. Her eyes instantly locked on Caedon, who was clearly caught off guard by her abrupt turn.

The duchess had already entered the dining wing. Caedon's eyes looked toward the stables, causing Luna's gaze to follow before flashing to the ground in embarrassment. When she peered up through her eyelashes, Caedon's mouth seemed to be holding back an amused smirk.

Both abashed and annoyed by this, Luna slid her shawl off her head, mustering a small bit of pride, and walked calmly to the door of the servants' wing. When she glanced to her right again, no one was there.

Chapter 5

It was a Wednesday and Luna had finally been able to spare some time to take her earnings back to Dirdra and Regan. It felt good to have a pouch full of enough currency to last them several weeks.

She prepared to leave, slipping on an eggshell bodice and meticulously lacing it up while standing in front of a full-length mirror. She was no longer in mourning, yet it felt odd to wear anything but black. She gathered the fabric of her earthy, brown skirt and left, hoping to slip out unnoticed. She had already told Katrin where she was going.

As she walked to her carriage, the hair on her arms and the back of her neck stood up, followed by a flourish of goosebumps. She felt a gaze upon her and turned around just before stepping into the carriage. Her eyes met those of a stranger, though it was not hard to deduce he was Caedon's younger brother by the familiar jawline and nose. His eyes, however, were a deep brown, dull in contrast to Caedon's.

He was walking the grounds with another man Luna did not recognize, though it was most likely one of the king's other guests. The other man was distracted, but Darius continued to stare, his penetrating eyes instantly turning Luna's stomach. She had experienced this feeling many times, but this time, perhaps, was the worst. Bringing a hand up to her mouth, she pressed a black lace handkerchief she had pulled from her pocket against her lips to stifle the nausea and turned to hoist herself into the carriage.

Once out of his view, Luna slowly exhaled, allowing her racing heart to ease and her skin to cool. It baffled her how differently each person's presence could feel. She shook her head and continued toward the manor.

Dirdra greeted her with a fresh pot of potato soup and baked bread. The instant Luna's feet crossed the threshold, she felt warm inside, a feeling she hadn't realized was missing until that moment.

The soup was thick and perfectly seasoned. Luna enjoyed the gentle heat as it settled in her stomach.

Both Dirdra and Regan were happy to see Luna, but they were also relieved to see the money. After discussing how it should be spent and catching up with both women, Luna prepared to leave. Though she had more than enough to eat at the castle, tradition never faltered. Dirdra wrapped a loaf of bread and filled a basket with fruit, some candles and herbs.

She also handed Luna's mother's medallion to her. Passed down through many generations of women, the crescent Triple Goddess symbol represented the three phases of the moon, as well as the three aspects of womanhood. Luna had not worn it since her mother's death, but she always kept it nearby, save for the past month.

She squeezed it inside her palm and nodded at Dirdra, whose eyes began to glisten from the emotion she saw in Luna's grateful gaze. She transferred the necklace to her now empty pouch and stepped outside, taken aback by how late it had gotten. The sun had already set, leaving a fuchsia sky in its wake and the vague twinkling of fast approaching stars.

Luna lit the lantern on her carriage and instructed the horse to go. As she made her way through the forested area of the path, however, she grew anxious. Her fingers instinctively tightened their grasp on the bar in front of her. The carriage hit a large hole, causing the wheel to crack and the cart to lurch forward. The spooked horse whinnied but could go nowhere.

Luna softly shushed her while she climbed forward and gingerly got out. No one was on the path, but she hoped someone would come by soon. Sure enough, Luna soon saw a lantern's dim light in the distance. As it approached, she straightened up and stood on the side of the path. She squinted and realized the traveler was riding on horseback.

The man gruffly commanded his horse to halt and Luna recognized him immediately as a gypsy. The more she examined him, his torn clothes, scraggly salt and pepper whiskers and unkempt hair, the sooner she realized he was a man familiar to the village. Regan had told Luna about him right before she started working with Katrin. Village gossip revealed that for one reason or another, the group he had traveled with shunned him and they had left him to fend for himself.

In light of her mother, and the very blood flowing through her veins, Luna carried a respect for most gypsies. However, her skin had already begun to tighten with goosebumps, drawing immediate caution.

The man saw her predicament, but his attention appeared to be caught by the inside of the carriage rather than the wheel and exasperated horse.

"Sir, if I could just have a hand in unhinging the horse ... we can be on our way," Luna said softly.

The gypsy turned on her, as if he only just now realized her presence. His eyes soaked her in, making her stomach turn. But his interest still remained in the carriage.

"Is it just you here?" he grumbled. Luna said nothing, quietly praying someone else would come by. But her ears heard nothing, save for the chirping crickets oblivious to her dilemma.

The man moved toward the carriage and began removing the bread and fruit basket. Luna decided it was nothing she couldn't part with as long as he left her alone. But her mind was too hasty to assume the worst was over. He then locked his eyes on her.

As he moved toward her, a slight breeze carried his rancid stench to Luna's nose, making her queasy and lightheaded. At first, she thought he had vulgar intentions. However, she swiftly realized his eyes were fixed on the pouch she had in her hand.

My mother's medallion.

"I have nothing of value Sir ... I just returned from the village where I emptied it," Luna said, clenching the pouch in her hand. "Please, do not come near me. If you must take the food, take it, but do not come near me."

Her words fell on deaf ears as the man stepped closer, now only a few feet away. He reached forward, grabbing for the pouch, but

Luna evaded him and began to run into the woods. She had no idea where she was going, but she knew she had to get away from him. To her surprise, the old man was quick on his feet, gaining on her. He grabbed her sleeve and ripped it, then snatched her skirt and tore that as well, but Luna kept moving until he grabbed a handful of her hair.

Her head snapped backward as she lost her balance and fell to the ground, her back ramming into his shins. He bent down to snatch the pouch, but Luna pulled it against her breast, curling her body around it. She felt something snap inside her, or perhaps it was more of an unfurling. Her skin began to smolder, but this time she felt no inhibitions to squelch it.

The man was completely unaware of what was transpiring as he groaned in frustration, trying to pry her arms apart. After a few minutes, it seemed to become a vendetta for him. His face was crimson with fury. He brought his fist down on her chest and breastbone multiple times, causing her to cry out in pain before he began to choke her. Her eyes – black with adrenaline and the hint of something sinister – locked onto his. What he saw in them made his hands slightly give on her throat, allowing a small stream of air through.

Her vision blurred around the edges, making the gypsy's head appear as though inside a tunnel. His face morphed into an ugly expression of agony and his breath caught. It was then Luna found movement and brought her right hand to his wrist, still clinging to her neck. The moment her hand touched his skin, he cried out in anguish and his wrist turned a deep red. It happened so fast, yet Luna could swear she saw the slightest movement under his skin, as though something was bubbling beneath its surface. His body went stiff and then barreled backward to the ground.

Gasping for breath, Luna crawled backward and scrambled to her feet, shaking. She entered a dizzy spell and felt her vision fading, but she continued to suck in lungful after lungful of air until her heart ceased racing and her drenched body cooled and stopped trembling. Her lips, an even deeper shade of plum, quivered as she shuffled closer to the still form on the ground. She did not have to check his pulse to know he was dead. He had the same placid eyes her father had in the end.

She shuddered, unsure of what to do, but quite convinced his heart had given out from the strain. Yet, the shadowy presence lurking inside her planted doubt.

Luna's eyes flashed to her hands and she slowly shook her head.

Impossible.

She decided it was time to leave. She checked the area as best she could under the waning light, making sure nothing of hers, not even a shred of her clothing, was left on the ground, and then ran back to the carriage. After grabbing her belongings, she worked on the harness of the horse and finally unhooked her. Hoisting herself up, she grabbed the reins and took off toward the castle.

This time, she prayed no one would pass by.

Chapter 6

It felt like hours had passed by the time Luna arrived at the gates. The soldiers, while maintaining their usual expressionless stance, could see Luna was in distress.

"Excuse me, my, my carriage ..." she stammered, but could hardly catch her breath. The guard quickly opened the gate for her. She slid off the back of the horse as one of the other men stepped forward to help her with her things.

"No, no. I don't need help. I just need to let you know that my carriage broke down back there, so I had to ride horseback the rest of the way. But it's still in the road," she said, her mind flashing back to the man in the woods.

"Okay, one of our men will fetch it," the guard said curtly. "Do you want one of us to take the horse?"

"No, I'll take her," Luna said hurriedly, moving past the gates while holding the horse's reins.

She made her way to the servants' stables, muffling her sounds as much as possible. After leaving the barn, she went over to the well. Thankfully, someone had left a wooden bucket resting against the stone siding. Luna lowered it into the well and brought it up quickly, pausing as she caught her reflection in the moonlit water.

She saw a hint of something glowing in her eyes before it slowly faded, like the embers of a smothered fire. Icy fear seeped into her veins.

What am I?

Without a second thought, she thrust her arms into the bucket and drowned her face in two handfuls of cold water.

They must get that carriage out of the way before someone finds him.

While repetitiously washing her face and hands, Luna's mind tangled up in a myriad of racing thoughts, so much so, she did not even notice a gentle touch on her shoulder.

"Are you okay?" a voice said, slicing through her trance. She looked up and into a pair of cobalt irises.

Caedon stepped back, catching a glimpse of Luna's stormy eyes. Knowing she needed to collect herself and do so quickly, she took a few deep breaths, pictured her father's calming eyes – so strikingly similar to Caedon's – and stood up.

His eyes skimmed over her, pausing on her arm, where her sleeve had been ripped, and then again at thigh level, where her skirt was torn. Her hair was in a long French braid, though it must have looked dreadful.

Seeing something change in her eyes, Caedon moved forward, but Luna threw her hands up, halting him.

"I'm okay. I was on my way back from my village. I was taking my earnings to my, to my ... family. And by the time I left, it was much later than I thought. I could hardly see the road and must have hit a large divot or hole, I am not sure, but the carriage broke down near the woods. I just do not want to cause any trouble and am worried it could cause another accident in the middle of the road," she said, realizing she was nervously babbling. Caedon picked up on it, too, and slowly raised his own hands as if to calm her down.

"I will see if we can get a couple of men to pick it up," he said reassuringly.

But Luna was not convinced, and Caedon could sense it.

"Come with me," he said. "Just for a few moments."

Hesitantly, Luna followed as Caedon walked back to the front gates. She subconsciously touched her hair, feeling several strands undone. The guards straightened up as Caedon approached.

"Your Grace," one of them said, giving a slight nod. Luna recognized him as the one who addressed her earlier.

"Yes. Send a few men over to ... " Caedon looked at Luna. "Where was this?"

"In the wooded area just east of the market," she said softly, looking down to the ground. Caedon studied her a moment before turning his attention back to the guard.

"East of the market, near ... " once again, he glanced at Luna, who looked back up at the guard.

"Baylus Village," she said, her raspy voice much louder this time. The guard briskly nodded, then looked at Caedon.

"Certainly, Your Grace. I'll send them now."

Caedon nodded and turned back to Luna, whose stature completely transformed to one of relief as she watched the men leave.

"Thank you, Your Grace," she said. A moment later, her mouth curled into a smirk, causing Caedon's brow to crease with curiosity.

"I suppose we are no longer even now," she said.

Caedon's mouth eased into a smile, almost reaching his eyes. Luna felt smiling was not something he did often.

"Perhaps we may consider it even if you would be so kind as to give me your name," he said.

Luna paused, still smiling. Though it quickly disappeared as she realized he was serious. The son of a duke wanting to know the name of a lowly servant girl seemed curious. It was one thing to know the name of a personal servant or handmaid, but this was uncommon.

"Luna," she said, never breaking contact with his eyes.

"Luna," he mumbled, trying it out on his lips as if tasting a new recipe. He nodded, seemingly satisfied, and then looked around him, suddenly aware of the remaining guards who were awkwardly trying not to look over at them.

Sensing his unease, Luna quickly bowed and began to retreat to the servants' wing.

Caedon remained in place, still as a statue, watching her disappear into the shadows.

*****

"Luna. Wake up. We must start early today. Have you forgotten?" Katrin's voice bellowed.

She rubbed her eyes and looked around the room, briefly disoriented. Sluggishly, she rose to her feet and cracked open the door to Katrin's strained face.

"His Highness is holding a ball for his guests this weekend," she said, making a tsk-tsk sound at Luna's appearance.

"Oh, oh yes. Right. I remember. I'm so sorry Katrin, I overslept," she replied, clearing her parched throat. "I did not get to bed until very late."

"I know. I was worried about you. I was going to send someone after you but thought perhaps you had just lost track of the time."

"Yes, I did lose track of time ... and had carriage trouble along the way," Luna said, swallowing the lump rising in her throat. "But all is well and I will be ready to go in a few moments."

Luna changed into her work clothes and headed out to meet Katrin in the linens room. She already had a large wooden cart filled with tablecloths. They rolled it to the lift and neatly stacked the folded cloths.

Shortly after, they were on the main floor where the ballroom was. Luna had only caught a glimpse of the ballroom since her stay. It was magical. The windows were narrow but reached to the ceiling. Marble columns surrounded the rectangular room, a fitting accent to the floor tiles, painted to match the design. The intricate woodwork on the tables and chairs was breathtaking. But the gothic limestone fireplace mantels captured Luna's particular interest. As she went by each one to light candles, she was captivated by their elaborate designs.

Suddenly, she heard Katrin and the other servants abruptly stop what they were doing. She turned around to see the two heavy wooden doors being pulled open and a man in the most stately attire she had ever witnessed walk in.

King Bertrem.

He was not a particularly handsome man. His hair was dark, with silver on the edges, framing a high forehead, sharp cheekbones and a prevalent nose. But his regal strides, healthy build and commanding presence were charismatic indeed. He was adorned in silks of crimson and gold so rich, Luna could barely keep from staring at them.

Along with everyone else in the room, Luna bowed, casting her eyes quickly to the ground. It seemed as though he was just passing through and wanted to check on how the décor was coming along. He looked at the tables, centered with aromatic oils, candles and freshly picked roses.

He only made eye contact with the four men in his company. Next to him, Duke Nicolai walked, complimenting the furnishings. Behind them, Caedon, Darius and the man Luna had seen walking with Darius yesterday afternoon sauntered in. Luna watched as Darius pushed past both men and walked in front of them, his chin defiantly lifted as he focused on the king and duke. Caedon and the other man quickened their pace but made no effort to join him.

Luna's keen awareness of body language sensed the visible tension between the brothers. They did not address each other; rather, they used the third man as a buffer. She might be assuming, but this seemed to be an age-old conflict that ran through very deep waters.

The men were approaching the opposite end of the room when Caedon glanced sideways, realizing Luna's presence. Her upper body still leaned slightly forward in a half-bow, her legs bent and hands grasping the folds of her skirt to steady her nerves. She looked up through her eyelashes and caught his look, sending a strange tickling feeling through her stomach, something she'd never experienced before. Her skin began to heat up. However, it was a gentle warmth, akin to the kind her father and mother used to invoke when they would look at her in adoration.

The feeling did not last, however, as a wave of icy chills rolled through her bones when her eyes shifted to another pair boring into her. Caedon's perceptivity never faltered. He noticed her body go rigid and followed her gaze to his brother.

After a few stealth paces, Caedon was within his brother's line of vision. He glared at him until Darius broke his stare and met Caedon's eyes, then quickly looked away.

Two servants heaved the doors open for the party to exit, the room already an afterthought. Luna straightened up, her legs a bit shaky, and grabbed a corner of the mantel for support as she watched their backs recede into the hallway. Only one pair of eyes turned back for a moment. The color of a cloudless sky, they briefly found hers, cut off only by the closing doors.

Chapter 7

The ball included the king's court, as well as several other dukes, duchesses, baronets, counts and knights. Mirium and the rest of her staff cooked a lavish dinner – a chicken broth and dumpling soup, fresh baked bread, sweet potatoes, crisp vegetables from the market and duck as the main course. The delectable aromas wafted throughout the servants' wing, causing Luna's stomach to grumble.

With all the extra chores on account of the evening's festivities, eating had completely evaded her. She was just about to make her way to the kitchen for some bread and soup when Katrin stopped her in front of the entrance.

"Luna. I know you have worked tirelessly today and I am grateful for the help," she began.

"What is it you need?" Luna asked, hunger wearing on her nerves.

"I need you to help Arianna with replacing a few of the candles that have burned out on the mantelpieces in the ballroom," she said distractedly, her thoughts already on a new task.

Luna nodded, grabbed a few bundles of burgundy tapered candles from a nearby cabinet and started toward the stairs. Briefly straightening her bodice and tucking a few loose strands of hair behind her ears as she approached the ballroom, Luna entered through the discrete servant door in the corner of the room.

Despite her expectations of a room brimming with magnanimity and nobility, her breath was stolen by the view before her eyes. Standing quietly in the shadows of the corner, Luna gazed around the room ignited by music, dancing, exuberant garments flooded with rich colors, gaiety and laughter. Burnished candelabras hung from the ceiling along with several candle sconces aligning the walls. Seeing the radiant fixtures reminded Luna why she was there.

She spotted Arianna near the middle mantelpiece. Looking around at the other five mantelpieces, she saw Arianna had already replaced three of them, leaving two that needed tending. Squeezing the candles in her right hand, she moved toward the nearest mantel on her side of the room. Making her way along the wall, she sensed eyes on her, but did not need to look to know who they belonged to. A soft warmth flooded her stomach.

She kept her eyes fixed on the mantelpiece in front of her. Quickly, she replaced two candles that were nothing but lumps of deformed wax. She then made her way to the last fireplace.

A swirling couple caught the corner of her vision, causing her to glance up. She saw Caedon dancing with a gloriously clad woman she presumed to be Duchess Rosalind. Her exquisite, champagne-colored gown flowed from her waist in layers of fabric. Luna's eyes shifted to Darius, who was standing adjacent to the fireplace Luna was in front of, conversing with a man she guessed to be a count or duke by his attire.

Darius' eyes were darker than she recalled. He seemed bored with the conversation, and occasionally yet pointedly looked over at his brother, resentment clear in his rigid features. Something the other man said caught Darius' attention, but it was fleeting. Within moments, the same detached manner returned, until his eye caught Luna's. She swiftly turned around to finish replacing the last two candles, but the fast motion, lack of sustenance and overall anxiety from the crowd dizzied her. Her knees began to buckle as she caught herself on the edge of the mantelpiece, feeling a strong hand grab under her other elbow.

She turned to face Darius. He was so close she could smell the wine on his breath.

"Are you alright?" he asked. His voice feigned gentleness, yet something dark laced every syllable.

Luna shook her head lightly and focused on his left shoulder instead of his eyes.

"Yes. Thank you, Your Grace," she said curtly, pulling away from his grasp.

Out of the corner of her eye, Luna saw Caedon. She realized he had watched the exchange. She grew embarrassed about becoming faint and immediately sought the exit. However, Darius remained in her way, his sooty eyes wandering the length of her.

"Excuse me, Your Grace," she said. He stood there a moment longer, dominating her space and her path to the door. At this point, the dance was over and she felt Caedon and the duchess approaching them.

"My, my Darius, are female partners so scarce, you've resorted to conversing with servants?" the duchess teased. Luna's skin began to tingle.

"Forgive me, Duchess Rosalind, if my brother occupies the prettiest woman in the room," Darius said, glancing at Caedon with narrowed eyes. Luna shifted uncomfortably, bringing everyone's attention back to her as she looked down at the floor.

"Can you not see? You are making the poor girl uncomfortable," the duchess said, though her tone conveyed no real concern.

Momentarily forgetting herself, Luna straightened her shoulders and looked up at the duchess, meeting her pale green eyes defiantly. Caedon, who was silently observing them, looked from Luna to the duchess, who seemed at a loss for words.

Whether from sheer disdain of being so close to his brother or the fact he grew easily bored, Darius stepped aside and offered his hand to the duchess, requesting the next dance. The proposition broke her focus on Luna. She softly smiled at Caedon before turning toward the crowd.

Caedon smiled back and slightly bowed forward, though his face grew solemn when he glanced up and saw his brother's devious smirk. Luna began to move toward the servant door when she felt a gentle touch on her elbow.

"Are you alright? I saw you almost took a fall before," he said in a low voice only she could make out.

"Yes. I'm fine. I just need to eat something. I am sorry my dizzy spell became such a spectacle."

"Nonsense. No one noticed but us."

Luna then realized Caedon had not removed his hand from her elbow. He looked down and quickly pulled it back. Her face became flushed, causing the corners of Caedon's mouth to twitch, as if repressing a grin.

What is wrong with me? Why can I not compose myself?

She blamed it on her increasing hunger, the exhausting day and the overcrowded room. But as Caedon took a step closer, there was no muffling the sound of her sharp inhale. The fluttering beat of her heart pounded in her ears as she heard him audibly take a deep breath in, his eyes closing.

Luna stole the moment to slip away. She glanced back only once before exiting through the door, astonished to find Caedon in the same position, his eyes still closed and a slight smile upon his lips.

Chapter 8

It had been days since the ball but Luna could not tear her thoughts away from the exchange she'd had with the duke's sons. Her skin crawled every time she pictured Darius blocking her path. His scent, stale with wine, permeated every breath she took.

But then her mind would turn to Caedon and his genuine concern, his engaging eyes and the way he had breathed her in, as if momentarily under a spell. It was such an intimate, yet completely inappropriate gesture given her station and the fact he is clearly promised to another. Luna shook her head and continued her walk to the village to bring last month's earnings to Dirdra and Regan.

She shuddered as she passed the spot where her carriage had broken down. She was certain by now someone had discovered the old man, but the memory still haunted her. Finally she made it to the manor. Dirdra, as always, had something cooking in the oven. This time, it was baked chicken.

"Luna! My heavens, you look paler than usual. Are you feeling well?" she said, pressing the back of her hand against Luna's forehead.

"I'm well, just a bit tired from the walk. I left the carriage at the market, desiring some fresh air," she feigned, knowing her ashen skin had more to do with a memory best kept buried.

"Well, sit down for some chicken and vegetables," Dirdra said, pulling out a chair for Luna. Regan strolled in with a basket of flowers, which she immediately set down after spotting Luna.

"Luna! I forgot you were coming this early," she said, smiling from ear to ear, her chocolate brown eyes seeming to instantly brighten. She gave Luna a tight hug, stood back and examined her a bit, then smirked.

"What?" said a suddenly self-conscious Luna.

"Nothing," Regan said, her tone a bit playful as her grin remained in place. Then, as if recalling something she'd been waiting forever to talk about, she sucked in a quick breath.

"Guess what?" she whispered, leaning forward conspiratorially.

"What?" Luna coaxed, teasingly rolling her eyes.

"A couple of kids were running in the woods a few weeks back and discovered a body," she said, dramatically pausing. While Luna did not have a mirror to illustrate, she was sure her face resembled the white tablecloth beneath her fingertips. However, Regan paid no attention, too caught up in her delivery.

"Guess whose body it was?"

Luna only nodded slightly, unable to speak, but Regan took it as a sign to go on.

"That old gypsy I was telling you about months ago. Remember?"

Luna nodded again.

"So anyway, the magistrate said it appears he died of natural causes, but I heard from Aeron – who delivers goods to his house and often overhears conversations she ought not to – that there seemed something suspicious about the circumstances, but nothing the magistrate could readily put his finger on."

Luna intently stared at her fingers now, as they slowly, methodically clenched and unclenched the cloth.

"However, I imagine because he's just a gypsy with no family or even friends in this area, the magistrate did not feel the need to waste any more time on him. Sad to say, but it makes sense," she said, a sudden note of sympathy in her voice. It was then she seemed to notice Luna's tense body.

"What's wrong?"

"Oh, nothing," Luna said, recovering quickly. She realized she was getting better and better at regaining composure these days.

"It's just a sad story. Did the magistrate say anything more about what exactly was suspicious?"

Regan paused for a moment, examining Luna's face, then, as if snapping out of a daydream, she slightly shook her head and continued.

"Though it appears his heart gave out on him, Aeron said he was tightly clasping his right wrist when they found him. And there was a strange, almost hand-shaped burn mark on his wrist. The magistrate thought perhaps something might have triggered a heart attack, that there were signs of a struggle of some sort. That and they found a small scrap of cloth in his right hand."

Luna felt her heart jump, though she maintained steady breathing.

"Unless someone saw something – which, no one has come forward so far – he said he would maintain it was a death by natural causes."

Luna's heart began to slow as she reminded herself she had nothing to fear. She shook her head, acknowledging the strangeness of the story and then changed the subject to something she knew would intrigue Regan.

"I saw the king."

Regan's eyes instantly locked on hers.

"It was as we were preparing for the ball. He walked through with a few men in his party and he looked magnificent," Luna said.

"Is that what I saw in your eyes when you first walked in?" Regan said, smiling wide.

"Perhaps," she said, though she believed Regan had seen the remnants of her last encounter with Caedon, which continued to dance upon the edges of her thoughts.

Luna described what she saw when changing out the candles, leaving out, of course, her conversation with Darius and Caedon. For some reason, as much as she loved and trusted Regan with her life, she felt the need to keep that part to herself. Dirdra hummed in the background, hustling around the kitchen as Luna and Regan conversed.

This time, making sure to leave well before nightfall, Luna made her way back to the market, a basket containing the blossoms and daisies Regan had picked as well as a fresh loaf of bread from Dirdra in hand. She chose to take a detour around the woods. It would mean a half hour more of walking, but that did not stop her in the slightest.

*****

A loud crack shook Luna awake. She sprung up to a seated position just as three flashes of lightning invaded her bedroom. Her parched throat felt like sandpaper. She looked over and frowned as she realized her cup of water was empty. Grabbing it, she tiptoed out into the hallway, hoping there was still some well water left in the kitchen from the bucket she had grabbed earlier.

Wind whistled past the windows, like a low agonizing scream. Luna wasn't scared, however. She enjoyed the sound as a child and it brought her comfort. As she walked through the kitchen, she spotted the bucket and sighed in relief when she saw there was some water left. Guzzling it down so quickly her head hurt, Luna let out another long sigh, this one in satisfaction. She closed her eyes and smiled, enjoying the simple moment of contentment.

Her expression changed, however, as she strained to hear what at first sounded like the crying wind, but quickly revealed itself to be the sound of a woman's panicked voice. It was coming from the other side of the kitchen door that led into a sitting room, one of the smaller parlors in that wing of the castle.

Luna quietly made her way to the door, which was slightly ajar. She peered through the crack and saw a man's form standing in the corner, barely visible from the low burning candles on the mantelpiece to his left. She heard whimpering coming from in front of him and looked down to see a pair of petite female feet facing his. Though he was standing in front of the woman, Luna was fairly certain it was Arianna.

Knowing she could not leave her, Luna deliberated her next move. She could wake Katrin or one of the other male servants, but that would cause more of a scene. Perhaps alerting this man of another person's presence would be enough to scare him off, she thought, nodding her head as she decided on this course of action.

She opened the door, knowing it would creak loud enough to be heard at the other end of the room. The man immediately backed away, revealing a terrified, half-dressed Arianna in the dim candlelight. She quickly covered herself and tried to sneak past him as he turned toward the door, squinting at Luna's silhouette.

"Who's there?" he said, his voice giving him away. Luna's abdomen tightened, her hands rolling into fists at her side.

She wanted to keep Darius distracted long enough for Arianna to escape, so she decided to step forward, the floorboards groaning beneath her bare feet.

"I said who's there?" he demanded. Arianna slowly moved along the wall toward the door on her left. She was only a couple feet away from escape.

Though Luna could smell the whiskey emanating from Darius, his reflexes were still impressively fast as he caught Arianna's moving form out of the corner of his eye.

"Excuse me, my dear, but we weren't finished," he said, causing her to stop in her tracks, her eyes wide as her legs visibly trembled.

"Leave her alone," Luna finally spoke, knowing she was taking a huge risk. But it worked. Darius' attention was caught. Arianna fled the room, throwing a grateful but worried look Luna's way before exiting.

He slowly sauntered toward her, swaying slightly, but somehow maintaining an arrogant posture. She began to back up toward the door, knowing once she was inside the kitchen, she would be able to run to her bedroom and lock him out. However, Darius was closing in quickly.

Her searching hand felt the cool brass knob behind her. She twisted it, but Darius grabbed her wrist just as she turned to flee. His strength was remarkable, as in one quick movement, he yanked her toward him and pushed her into another corner of the room. Her head lightly bumped against the wall and she instinctively brought her hand to the back of it. Darius, still holding her wrist, grabbed her raised hand and brought it down to her side, pinning it against the wall.

"Please. Just let me go," she whispered.

"You deprived me of my former distraction, so naturally, that puts you in quite a predicament," he said, his breath rank, reminding her of the damp, moldy insides of an old chest. She held her breath as she flexed her arm muscles, trying out her strength against his. She found she was no match, however inebriated he might be.

"Feisty, I see. I like that," he purred, moving closer to her, his mouth by her ear. She felt his lower body press against hers. She squirmed away, but had nowhere to go. Her struggle seemed to only intensify his body's reaction as his breathing quickened against her temple.

"For an insignificant little maidservant, you smell absolutely delicious," he said. "And you feel even better. I could positively ravish those deep, sumptuous lips."

Luna felt as though she would retch right in his face.

"Let me go. Now," she growled.

He paused for a moment, his lethargic eyes narrowing at something he saw in hers. But whatever it was seemed to arouse him more, his mouth spreading into a malicious grin.

"Do not ever give *me* orders," he said, though his tone conveyed mocking.

Luna closed her eyes and tried to clear her thoughts. She felt her skin crawling from his touch, from his energy. And though chills scampered down her spine, her flesh began to simmer. Darius was oblivious, his eyes filling with nothing but the desire to consume her.

Her knee was preparing to strike him in the groin. However, just as his mouth closed in on hers, she heard a sharp voice behind them.

"Darius."

His lips, merely centimeters from hers, pulled back into a grimace.

"Leave me," he simply said, keeping his eyes locked on Luna, who was now frozen in place by the sound of Caedon's low, composed voice.

"I will not," he answered, just as simply.

Darius scowled and turned his head to glare at his brother, who now caught a glimpse of Luna's brooding face. Caedon's eyes widened a bit, then seemed to harden into stone. Darius continued to glower at his brother, flabbergasted by his refusal to leave. Luna had a feeling this was not the first of these encounters.

"You are intoxicated, Darius. Need I remind you why you should know better than to take advantage of a servant, no less one who works for King Bertrem. Just go to bed," he said in disgust.

Luna sensed no brotherly feelings between the two at all now that she was completely alone with them.

"I'm sorry, when did you take father's place?" Darius snapped, his menacing eyes growing darker. Caedon took a step closer, though he continued to remain reserved and in control.

Luna decided to take advantage of the interlude, jerking her knee upward. It struck its intended target, causing Darius to keel over in anguish.

"You nasty little bitch," he snarled, though Caedon had already stepped forward and grabbed Darius under both arms from behind.

Luna fought the urge to counter his verbal attack, deciding against it when her eyes met Caedon's, which were begging her to remain silent.

After a few moments, Darius seemed to reassess the situation and let his body grow lax.

"I'm fine," he said, pushing back against Caedon, who let him go. Embarrassed he had lost his temper in front of his brother, as well as Luna, he straightened up, his expression transforming before their eyes.

He turned toward his brother, lifting his chest and raising his chin up as he met Caedon's steady gaze.

"You always manage to spoil my fun ... brother," he said, sarcasm dripping. He then turned back to Luna, who met his eyes straight on, and huffed as if to say she was now an afterthought.

He left through the door on the opposite end of the room. Caedon watched after him for a few moments, listening to his retreating, stumbling footsteps before turning his eyes to Luna.

"I would ask you, for what seems like the millionth time, if you are alright, but it seems as though you had yourself handled," he said, trying to make light of the situation.

Luna let out a small, nervous laugh.

"Hardly," she said, shaking her head ruefully. "I hadn't thought past the kneeing."

Caedon's composure crumbled as he let out a laugh. It was rich and warm and filled the room. This time, his smile met his eyes, causing them to glimmer in the faint candlelight. Luna found herself laughing as well, though hers sounded more hysterical, perhaps the result of frayed nerves.

Caedon seemed to pick up on it and grew solemn again.

"I'm very sorry," he said, looking as though he wanted to say more, perhaps to explain his brother's actions, but came up empty. "I'm just … sorry."

Luna nodded, but his apology did not make her feel any better. The tension in her muscles caused them to atrophy as her body began to shut down. She started to sink to the floor, but Caedon was at her side within seconds. He grabbed her, lifted her body fluidly into his arms and took her over to a nearby settee, propping her up against a few pillows.

The movement caused her scent to flood his nose as he knelt down beside her, feeling a bit lightheaded as well.

"I'm embarrassed," she said, looking down as she brought her left hand to her forehead. "It's like when a person drains all the energy they have in their body. Something just comes over me. Or rather … takes me over. But it happens so rarely."

Luna realized she was not only babbling, but speaking of things best left unspoken.

Caedon, however, stared at her in what could only be construed as fascination. This caused Luna to look down, unsure of what to do or say. Before she could utter another word, his warm hand gently wrapped around her frigid fingers. The touch caused a wave of immense warmth to flood her bones. Her heart picked up pace as she met his eyes, now only inches away from hers.

His other hand came up to the left side of her face, his thumb lightly grazing her cheekbone before his fingers softly entangled with the hair behind her ear. He leaned in slightly but dared go no farther. She felt a strange burning in her lower abdomen and limbs, causing her breath to quiver. Caedon slightly trembled in response. She leaned forward and pressed her lips into his.

Something inside her shifted again, though this time it felt like her heart. Her mouth pressed harder into his, making Caedon shiver even more. This amused her from a man who clearly takes pride in his equanimity. A raw, almost primal need overtook her, as her mouth moved in sync with his, slowly sliding down to envelope his lower lip with her teeth. This action took him off guard, causing Luna to pull back, embarrassment flooding her face.

The corners of his mouth pulled up into a sort of astonished smile. Luna's face felt flushed and her hands instinctively flew to her cheeks. Caedon studied her, his eyes moving over her distinct jawline, her forehead, lips, before locking back onto her eyes again. Suddenly, his disheveled demeanor altered into something more collected, though his features remained soft.

"Please forgive me," he said, his voice cracking slightly with emotion that took them both aback.

Perplexed, Luna stared at him for a few moments before she understood why he was asking for forgiveness. In fact, there were many reasons behind the apology, she realized, as the reality of what just occurred sank in.

"It's okay," she whispered, her voice weak from his lips. Though something inside her told her it was far from alright. Something had changed, and not just within her.

Caedon shook his head, as if reading her thoughts, or simply just angry with himself. He stood up and extended his hands, which she gently clasped before he pulled her swiftly to her feet. Placing his hand under her chin, he lifted her face to meet his eyes, examining her under the candlelight in such an intimate way, she felt more exposed than she ever had. Finally satisfied by what he saw, he dropped his hands and placed his left hand to the small of her back, guiding her toward the kitchen door. When she reached the door, he held it open for her but refused to meet her gaze.

She understood why, yet for some reason her heart felt the tightest pinch as he closed the door behind her.

Chapter 9

Sunday came around faster than anticipated and Luna found herself, once again, discomfited as she sat in a crowded pew at the chapel. With Katrin on one side and Mirium on the other, Luna had little room to move, much less breathe. Her heart remained steady, save for the few times she felt the priest's penetrating eyes on her. Never once did she look up, careful to keep her lashes lowered.

Finally, the sermon was over and everyone began to shuffle out. Luna noticed Mirium and Katrin talking to a few women she recognized from the market at the bottom of the steps. As she made her way to them, a hand suddenly grabbed her arm. She turned, standing face to face with the priest, who seemed to scrutinize her with his murky, sea green eyes.

"My apologies. I did not mean to startle you," he said. "I do not believe I've ever properly introduced myself. I am Father Geirnuk. Hans Geirnuk."

The name sent a flood of acidic saliva down Luna's throat. She thought he had looked familiar, but could not put her finger on it before.

His eyes were fixated on her forehead, as though concentrating on that part of her so as not to look elsewhere. She shuddered under his gaze, as his brow began to furrow. Her body, frozen in place, would not listen to her mind, which perilously begged it to move.

"Have we met before? I feel as though I've seen you before," he said, his eyes now beginning to scan the length of her.

She heard his breath pick up pace and could visibly see the pulse in his neck quicken. She knew if she did not leave in that moment, he would figure it out – a possibility she could not allow.

"What is your name dear?" he asked, still entranced by an unknown force Luna could not control. Before she could answer, she heard an all too familiar voice intercede.

"Hello, Father," Caedon said, his legs crossed as he casually leaned his right shoulder against the chapel entryway. Caedon's eyes locked on the surprised priest's eyes before darting down to where he still held Luna's arm.

Father Geirnuk swiftly withdrew his hand, like a naughty child caught stealing a piece of candy. He stepped back and seemed to regain his composure while Caedon straightened up and approached them both.

"Your Grace, forgive me. I was just introducing myself to ... some new blood in the parish," he said, his words sending a shiver down Luna's spine. Caedon studied the priest for a moment and then looked at Luna, sensing her disquiet.

"Ah, I see. Well, I'm here at the king's request to ask if you would be so kind as to hold a service next week for Lady Beatrice. She has fallen ill once again, this time ... much worse," he said, his expression suddenly dour.

"Yes, yes of course I will, Your Grace. Let His Majesty know I will hold a service next Sunday for her," he said, bowing before making his way to the altar. He only glanced back at Luna once, before catching Caedon's glare and quickly snapping his head forward.

Caedon extended his arm to Luna, whose nerves were rattled by the entire exchange, as well as his gesture to escort her. She heard Katrin and Mirium still prattling on outside and did not know what else to do except take his arm. She reticently wrapped her left arm around his, catching a slightly amused smirk on his face.

He leaned in, bringing his mouth inches from her ear.

"You have a very peculiar effect on people," he said, his breath upon her skin causing chills to scuttle down her spine.

"And you have an uncanny knack for showing up just in the knick of time," Luna quipped. Caedon let out a soft chuckle.

"Indeed, I seem to – at least with you."

Luna looked into his eyes, blushing at the intensity dancing in them. In all the times she had secretly stolen glances at him these past weeks, she had never seen depth quite like this in his eyes ... even when he looked at Duchess Rosalind. At this thought, Luna flushed even more, her normally porcelain skin a soft pink. Caedon's eyes flitted across her features before he put on his usual indifferent expression as they made their way outside.

"Luna dear, there you are," Katrin said, then immediately bowed after spotting Caedon. "Oh, Your Grace, forgive me, I did not see you there."

"It's perfectly fine Ms. Katrin. I was just delivering her to you," he said, causing Katrin's eyes to light up, surprised he knew her name. Luna was astonished as well, her mouth slightly agape. Caedon glanced at her and visibly repressed another grin. She conscientiously closed her mouth as Caedon released her from his grasp, seeming just as hesitant to do so as she was. The motion lingered, though no one seemed to notice, too caught up by Caedon's beautifully chiseled face and crisp attire.

Luna gracefully descended the stairs, softly landing right next to Mirium.

"Shall we?" Mirium said, looking at Katrin, who was still off kilter. The other two women from the market were standing next to them as well.

"Luna, you'll be able to squeeze in, won't you? There's a storm coming and we did not want to leave Arial and Constance to walk back to the village alone," Katrin said.

"That should be just fine, I could sit – "

"Or, the young lady could just ride with me, making it easier on everyone," Caedon interjected, causing the women's attention to snap back to him. Luna was speechless. Of course, no one would refuse this. It was logical and it was not in anyone's place to deny. The lot of them acquiesced this was the better arrangement and piled into the carriage with Caedon's appeasing assistance.

It was then Luna realized just how literal Caedon was when he said "ride." Standing to the right was a gorgeous silver stallion. Luna was slightly intimidated, but pride kept her from showing it.

"He's glorious," she said. "What is his name?"

"Libra."

Luna's heart jumped for reasons she could not fathom. She felt as though she had known this horse's name before. In fact, she also felt she had known this man standing unnervingly close to her long before now, as well.

She nodded, showing her approval of the name while noting a beguiled Caedon. Her blood warmed at how exasperated those smirks made her. He stepped in, preparing to lift her onto the horse. Her legs began to feel numb as his energy washed over her.

"May I?"

She swallowed and nodded, making his smile even larger. His warm hands cradled her sides just above her hips. She looked up, locking her silvery eyes on his. His smile quickly diminished as he stood perfectly still, time seeming to halt. Then, just as swiftly as the moment came, it passed and he hoisted her onto the magnificent creature, quickly following suit.

As they trotted off, neither one noticed a pair of green eyes meticulously studying the exchange through a stained glass chapel window.

*****

The ominous storm hovered over them as Caedon urged Libra from a trot to a canter. The gentle rocking motion caused Luna's back to fall in succession with Caedon's chest. A large thunder crashed, followed by several streaks of lightning. Luna barely flinched, as a mischievous smile spread across her lips. She loved summer storms. Caedon, who was prepared to reassure her, was taken by surprise at her smiling face and closed eyes. They continued on, just making it to the stables as a heavy downpour began. Though they made it inside the barn within moments, both Luna and Caedon were drenched.

Luna giggled, covering up her mortification at how dreadful she must look. She reached up to her hair and, feeling it was a matted mess, pulled out several pins. Her deep mahogany locks cascaded down her back and shoulders, causing Caedon, who had just secured Libra in his stall, to stop in his tracks.

"You are quite possibly the most exquisite creature I have ever encountered," he said to her, a rueful look on his face.

Luna's lips parted, straining for some kind of response, but she came up short. Caedon stood silently for a few moments, his eyes searching hers.

"I would have to say, Your Grace – "

"Caedon," he said gently.

"Caedon," Luna said, letting each syllable roll over her tongue, unsure of herself. "I would have to say I am deeply honored by your compliment, but am quite baffled not only by what you see, but why you see it."

Caedon examined her for a few moments, realizing in her eyes that she, indeed, was oblivious to her mystifying beauty. He also did not have to read her thoughts to know she was referring to Duchess Rosalind. He thought carefully before he spoke, taking another step toward her and eliciting a soft whinny from the mare behind.

"I feel as though I have known you before. The moment I saw you, I felt something stir within me. I have tirelessly tried to make sense of it to no avail."

Sensing he wanted to go on, Luna remained silent, though a hundred thoughts surreptitiously danced in her mind.

"I do not mean to cause any offense, but I have not conversed in any truly meaningful way with a servant since I was a child and not yet aware of the disparity between stations. My mother died when we were very young and my father has always been very – " Caedon paused, a dark emotion flashing across his face, "strict with us. He has always made sure we understood our position in life, as well as other people's positions and purposes. Those lines are never allowed to be crossed in his book."

Caedon moved another foot closer, bringing him inches from Luna's face. She took a deep breath, holding it as she waited for him to go on.

"But Luna," he said, basking in the sound of her name on his lips, "I am drawn to you. I have torturously fought it for weeks, ashamed of myself because of my promise to Duchess Rosalind. But something has shifted and I cannot seem to shift it back."

So many questions, so many consequences, so many dangers, yet

Luna could not utter a single word. Her heart throbbed furiously in her chest, causing her skin to burn up at an alarming rate.

In one rapid movement, her lips crashed against his, her hands grabbing the back of his head and neck, pulling his body against hers. He pushed into her, causing her to back up toward one of the stalls. Her skin smoldered, as she felt a strong yearning inside of her. She playfully, yet assertively pushed back, causing Caedon to pause, taken by surprise. He dove back into her lips, his tongue slowly yet hungrily intertwining with hers. He brought up his hand to her cheek and quickly pulled it back in shock.

"You are burning," he said, incredulously. "It's my fault ... the rain, you're soaked – "

Luna brought a finger to his lips, freezing him in place.

"I am feverish, but not for the reasons you fear," she said. Caedon sensed she chose her next words carefully.

"My ... body operates differently than most. Its temperature excites easily."

She stopped there, hoping that was enough. Caedon studied her a bit longer, seeming to see right through her, but he did not push. Luna had a distinct feeling he would never push.

He brought a hand gently to her temple, gingerly moving a strand of wet hair from her face. The tender motion made her cloudy, passion-filled eyes soften.

Caedon seemed transfixed by them, the infinite volumes they spoke.

"You might just be the death of me," he whispered.

Several yards away, a pair of dark, portentous eyes watched every movement as Luna ran through the drizzling rain to the servants' wing. But it was not until they caught sight of Caedon, exiting the very same stable, that they grew far more sinister.

Chapter 10

The dream was one Luna knew well. It was always the same scenario. Her mother had just left the church in their old village, a place so far away, yet its memory remains etched in her mind.

Cybele.

Derived from the goddess of fertility, her mother's name had not been uttered since that day. The lucidity of the nightmare always made Luna feel as though she were reliving the harrowing events.

Vividly, she watches as the chipped, wooden doors of the church fly open and her mother's figure steps out. She looks slightly crazed, her eyes glossed over with conflicting emotions. Luna feels a chill roll down her spine as she catches a glimpse of the deep-seated ire festering in her mother. Then, as her gaze finally brushes over Luna and Jevan, the anger slowly melts, giving way to deep heartbreak.

She walks slowly toward them, her feet grazing the dirt with each dazed step, until she is inches from Luna. Her eyes hesitantly lower, meeting Luna's penetrating gaze. They reveal a depth of love that pours into her, wrapping around her heart, before piercing anguish assails them.

Cybele raises her head slightly to look at Luna's father, tenderly touching his cheek. They simply stare into each other's eyes.

Luna was 12 years in age, not yet a woman, but her body had begun to flourish, as did its strange reactions to extreme emotion. She remembers clasping her mother's other hand, her eyes searching for answers, for assurance, but her stomach violently drops when she finds none.

Luna's mind shifted away from the dream a moment, recalling how she and her mother had just spent that previous evening together, something they had not done in months. Cybele, with an air of foreboding surrounding her, told Luna things she had no real understanding of at that age.

"Luna, listen to me. I'm not sure what tomorrow will bring. But

I want you to always be cautious, to continuously practice peace within yourself, for you know what happens when you don't have inner peace, yes?"

Luna, her eyelids brimming with tears, only nodded.

"You must remember that people will never understand you. And that is alright. But what people do not understand, they fear, just as they fear me. So, it is important that you and your father strive to remain in the shadows, to fit in. I'm afraid many things will change after tomorrow. What those changes will be, I do not yet know."

"Mama," Luna had choked, taking in an unsteady breath. "Why are you talking as though you will not be with us?"

Her mother said nothing, but her striking gypsy green eyes had said everything, and it was then, Luna broke down. She remembers Cybele immediately wrapping her warm, safe arms around Luna, rocking her gently back and forth while humming, the way she did when she was a baby.

After what seemed like hours, her mother had whispered gently in Luna's ear.

"There are still many big things to come for you, my love. Some of them will be magical, intensely life changing, but I'm afraid the soul's ties to the past are out of your hands, Luna. Those ties are bound to another and I'm uncertain where they will lead this time. I cannot see it. I wish I could, so that I may help you in some way, any way ..."

She trailed off, and though Luna had heard every word, their meaning had remained a mystery.

None of that mattered that following day. As Luna's thoughts return back to the nightmare, she remembers the only thing at the forefront of her mind was the tormented, terrified look in her mother's eyes. Her beautiful olive skin, tear-streaked as she stood in stark contrast next to Luna's fair-skinned father.

This part of the dream always blurs a bit, yet Luna never forgets the feeling of her mother fiercely pulling her into a hug, so tight she could almost feel her bones break. She remembers the priest, standing in the church entryway, his murky, pale green eyes narrowing as he watches the exchange. And she never forgets the two assistant magistrates, standing close by, waiting, and finally walking over to pry Luna from Cybele's arms.

"Lucinda. Remember the name Lucinda!" her mother screams to Luna's outstretched arms as Luna begs for the men to let her mother go. But that marked the last time she would see Cybele. Her father had restrained her and kept her in their home for the next three days.

Perhaps it had been just her vivid, morbid imagination, but on that third day, just hours before she and her father fled the village with Dirdra and Regan, Luna swore she had heard earsplitting screams from the village square, followed by a deafening silence.

*****

Luna shot up in her bed, heart racing and brow, neck and chest shimmering with sweat as she felt her damp clothes sticking to her limbs. Suddenly, her body felt cold as ice and she ripped every piece of clothing off, replacing them with a clean, dry, multilayered sage skirt and eggshell bodice. Working her hair into two loose braids that hung past each shoulder, she ran cold water over her face, attempting to wash away the lingering nightmare.

Katrin met her at the kitchen entrance, flushed from walking down the flights of stairs.

"Good morning, Luna. Will you help me with these bed linens for the women's quarters?"

Luna responded by grabbing several stacks of sheets out of Katrin's hands and following her up the stairs.

When they reached the first room, Katrin knocked lightly.

"Come in," said a soft voice, which Luna recognized as Duchess Rosalind.

They entered, bowing quickly in the duchess' direction before tending to the bed. Luna gave a sideways glance at the golden beauty as Arianna, who was already in the room, briskly worked her corset laces. The duchess was glorious, her skin pale with a slightly pink hue. All at once, Luna felt deflated, then she caught Arianna's eye and nodded at the unspoken words of gratitude they bestowed.

The memory instantly took Luna past the ugliness of Darius and into the clement arms of Caedon.

She blushed, pulled back to her task by Katrin clearing her throat. As they exited the room, the duchess, who saw them pass by in her mirror, abruptly turned around.

"It's you," she said in a tone of surprise.

Luna slowly turned around, feeling plainer than ever as she faced the duchess' flawless, delicate face.

"I hear my Caedon came to your rescue the other night," she said, emphasizing his name. "Darius is such a terrible drunk who often rambles on his way to bed. I do dread the day I must call him my brother-in-law."

Out of the corner of her eye, Luna watched Arianna noticeable stiffen at the mention of Darius, however, she kept her eyes trained on the duchess. Luna feigned an awkward smile, unsure of why the duchess felt the need to tell her any of this. Katrin stood in the doorway, her brow creased in confusion, though she remained silent.

"Well, I just wanted to apologize on behalf of Darius. He truly is a different, much more reserved man when he isn't drinking," she said, now seemingly embarrassed by her sudden discourse with Luna.

Luna and Katrin bowed once and left the room.

"What on earth was that all about?" Katrin said.

"Nothing. Just a mix up the other night when I was getting some water for my parched throat," Luna said, praying Katrin would leave it at that. And she did, reminding Luna again why she respected the woman so highly.

Luna and Katrin walked outside with a couple buckets, heading over to the well. Off in the distance, Luna heard a few voices near the king's gardens. She squinted, making out three men, but was only sure of one – Caedon. His stride was unmistakable to Luna.

"Katrin," she said, with as much nonchalance as she could muster. "The third man who often walks with His Graces' Darius and Caedon, pray what is his name?"

Katrin paused in the middle of hauling the overflowing bucket up the well and looked up at the sky, thinking.

"That is Lord Tamas. His wife, Lady Beatrice, has been quite ill and bedridden for some time," she said, frowning slightly before resuming her work. Luna helped her unlatch the bucket and clasp on another to lower into the well.

Luna remembered Caedon asking the priest to have a service for Lady Beatrice. The memory sent sudden chills down Luna's spine as the vision of a much younger Father Geirnuk standing in the church entryway in her dream flashed into her mind. She banished it quickly and looked back at Katrin.

"Also, I meant to ask you this before, but what did you say Caedon and Darius' mother's name was?" Luna asked, the same casual tone in her voice.

"Oh. Her name was Lucinda."

Chapter 11

It took every ounce of calm for Luna to maintain a mask of normalcy after that name vacated Katrin's mouth. Yet somehow, she managed. In fact, she made every effort to keep busy the rest of the evening so as not to let her assiduous mind ponder anything else but the tasks at hand.

It wasn't until the evening – a smoldering, sticky night as it was – that she finally loosened the knot around her racing thoughts. Was it merely an absurd coincidence? Or perhaps she had heard Katrin wrong. Perhaps because of the nightmare she'd had the day before, her mind was playing tricks on her. But she recalled watching Katrin mouth the name Lucinda.

But how? How could this be? How could a duchess have associated with the likes of my mother, a gypsy?

Sure, Cybele was not just any gypsy. She had married a fair-skinned peasant, much to their community's dismay and against all others' wishes. And yes, her father was a yeoman, owning his own land, but he was a commoner nonetheless.

No matter which way Luna laid out the pieces, none of it made sense. But somehow, someway, she knew she had to learn more about Lucinda. She was the key to solving the peculiar mystery of how their families were tied together, of why Luna feels such a connection, a familiarity around Caedon. Whatever the answer is, it fringed on something paramount. Luna felt it reverberate within her bones.

Pressing Katrin for more information was too risky. And Luna trusted no one else with such personal questions about a noble family. Well ... almost no one.

*****

Luna tried to be inconspicuous when asking Regan if she would walk the grounds of their manor with her a bit for fresh air. Dirdra, completely engrossed in housework, merely waved them away while continuing to scrub the kitchen counters. No one spoke for a full five minutes, though Luna could feel Regan's eyes piercing through her.

"When we were younger and mama – I mean, my mother was still alive, did you ever recall her saying the name Lucinda?"

Regan slowed her pace a bit, searching her memory while staring at her feet crunching over the stiff grass. Suddenly, her eyes widened in recognition.

"Yes. Once, while I was cleaning the hearth in your mother's room, I happened upon a letter she must have forgotten to stow away, for it was something intimate indeed," Regan said, blushing in embarrassment.

"I should not have looked. It was not my business, but I was young and did not know much better," she said, ruefully.

Luna shook her head, impatiently dismissing Regan's apologies and urging her to continue on.

"Anyhow, I remember it was addressed to a Lucinda Nicolai ... a Duchess Lucinda Nicolai," Regan said slowly, her eyes narrowing as she focused on the memory. "I don't remember everything, but the missus, I mean, your mother, was thanking the duchess for taking the time to meet with her as well as for her discretion. She seemed to be vague on purpose, but I remember the letter saying something along the lines of she feared she would never see the duchess again, but would never forget their bond."

Not realizing they both had stopped walking, Luna listened intently, utterly transfixed by Regan's words.

"Was this ..." but she could not say the words aloud and it did not take long for Regan to read her thoughts.

"Yes, this was not long before it," she said, her eyes dropping to the ground in sadness and respect.

"If you don't mind my asking, Luna, why do you ask?"

Luna stared at Regan a moment longer, deliberating how much to tell before deciding to give just enough to settle her curiosity.

She told her about the duke, his sons – though mentioned nothing about her encounters with Caedon – and about their mother, Lucinda, who had passed away from some type of lingering illness not long after Cybele. Regan saw right through some of Luna's pretenses, particularly when she mentioned Caedon's name. But for a change, she did not press her, just listened, nodded and studied Luna's face.

"Well, not that my word means much of anything, but I would have to say I agree with you about finding a way to discover more about Lucinda. Perhaps you can talk with one of the other servants who are familiar with the family," Regan said, raising her eyebrows.

But Luna tersely shook her head, causing Regan to furrow her brow once again in contemplation.

"I will figure something out, do not worry," Luna reassured her, then quickly changed the subject. "So, how are things here? Is everything running okay or do you need more of my wages a little earlier than usual?"

Regan filled her in on a few goings-on in the village, but assured her things at the manor were just fine. Luna half listened as they made their way back to the kitchen and Dirdra's rosy, overheated complexion.

*****

Once back at the king's estate, Luna finished the last load of linens and decided to take the air before the sun retired for the evening. She stepped outside and relaxed as a gentle, warm breeze brushed past her, fluttering her emerald peasant skirt. Much to her surprise, King Bertrem allowed servants to walk the gardens as long as it was in the latter portion of the evening.

However, this was her first visit and as soon as she crossed under the cast iron archway, she found herself engulfed by the most glorious garden she had ever witnessed. To her right were the exotics, the lilies, yuccas and irises. And to her left, the sweet aroma of blossoms and honeysuckle invaded her senses. She walked along the cobblestone path, completely mesmerized by the vast array of flower species the king had, many of them she had never laid eyes on before. She sat on a bench in front of a small display of vibrantly colored daisies.

Closing her eyes, Luna breathed in the mild, saccharine scent. Suddenly, as if overcome by the aromas and sensory stimulation, she grew drowsy. She curled up on the bench and decided to rest her eyes for a moment.

When she awoke, it was well past dusk and the stars had begun to shimmer. Luna rubbed her eyes and looked around, suddenly embarrassed and praying she did not get into trouble or had Katrin worried. Gathering her skirt, she stood up, a bit dizzy from the fast motion. Taking a moment to regain her bearings, Luna stood in place and took a few deep breaths, still overcome by the potency of aromas invading her senses. It was then she heard a footstep scuffling against the cobblestone. The hair on her neck and arms instantly stood on end as she felt a presence approach from behind her. Luna swallowed and slowly turned around.

"Well, well, well ... what have we here?" Darius cooed, though there was nothing endearing in his tone.

Luna looked to the ground, curtsied briefly and turned to walk toward the archway, now cloaked by violet shades of twilight. Darius did not grab her hard this time. He merely reached out, letting his hand encircle her upper arm and then graze down the length of it as she retreated, stopping at her fingers. She quickly pulled her arm away from him.

"Pray tell me, what is your name? I get the funny feeling my brother knows it and I cannot be having the flawless Caedon know something I do not," Darius said, dark sarcasm dripping from each syllable.

Luna visibly shuddered, causing Darius' lips to spread into a wider grimace.

"Your Grace, I really must be getting back or the head servant will start to look," Luna said calmly, hoping her words were enough to make Darius rethink whatever intentions he had formed. But it was to no avail.

Reaching back out and pulling her close to his chest with impressive force, Darius breathed her in. Her stomach churned as she watched his eyes roll back slightly.

"You know … I do believe – and correct me if perhaps my vision betrayed me – but I do believe I saw you leave the king's stables last week during that dreadful storm," he purred, bringing his lips close to her ear. "And if I am not mistaken, I thought I saw my brother vacate that same stable just moments later."

Luna audibly sucked in a breath and held it as her heart began to pound in her ears. Darius seemed to relish the effect he was having on her. She heard his own breath quicken slightly as his body stiffened.

"Now, what would the beautiful, sweet Duchess Rosalind think of such an odd coincidence, or perhaps King Bertrem himself?" Darius said, causing Luna to finally meet his eyes. At first, her pupils were wide with fear, but as she stared deeper into his, they narrowed, her irises clouding over.

"Yesss," he hissed, as if this was the very reaction he had hoped for. He seemed fascinated as he watched her eyes darken into a smoky ashy haze. But it was not just her eyes he focused on, she watched him noticeably glance down at the hand he still had gripping her arm. It was then, she realized what he felt – intense, fierce heat. He let go instinctively, but held her in place with his other hand on her shoulder. He stared down at his palm incredulously and then looked back up to Luna's penetrating gaze.

Suddenly, her father's eyes popped into her mind and she instantly began to slacken. Darius studied her. He saw her become calm again and decided to press her further. He stepped so close, his lips were mere inches from her forehead. A chill scampered down her spine as she tried to maintain inner tranquility. His stale, sour stench permeated every breath she took, causing her to suppress a gag. She held as frigidly still as a rabbit in front of prey. He tilted his head to the side and found her throat with his tongue. Slowly, he slid it up the length of her neck until he reached her earlobe, his saliva burning against her skin.

Reflexively, her hand met with his hard chest as she pushed back slightly to gain a few more inches between them. It was in that moment she heard horse hooves galloping past the garden and Katrin's voice calling her name at the same time.

Recognizing defeat, at least for now, Darius grunted in frustration, backed up and released her shoulder. He did not have to say anything. His veiled threat, if she uttered a word of this to anyone, was clear in his sable, ominous eyes. She fled through the archway, spotting Katrin by the well peering through the darkness in her general direction.

"I know, I know ... I'm so sorry. I fell asleep in the garden and lost track of the time. Please do not be angry," she pleaded when she was within hearing distance of Katrin.

"I was mostly just worried dear," she said, though her relieved expression quickly grew solemn. "And if King Bertrem were to find out about this, he would not be pleased."

Luna met Katrin's eyes and nodded briskly. Katrin left it at that and they retreated to the kitchen without another word. Luna was not positive, but she could have sworn she heard the low, familiar sound of Caedon's voice carrying over from the stables. Its stern tone was followed by the unmistakable growl of the man, who, just moments ago, had come very close to destroying her.

Chapter 12

Dreading Sunday morning's church service, Luna bit down on her lip while her carriage approached the solitaire stone chapel. Discreetly, she wiped her slightly swollen lip with a handkerchief and watched as the mist from the recent cool, dewy rain rolled past her lips. She shivered, then followed Katrin out of the carriage and onto the mushy ground.

They quietly entered just as Father Geirnuk began mass. He shot Katrin a fleeting glance, then gave a double look as Luna followed behind. His eyes locked with hers, gluing her to the floor at the center of the aisle. He paused between verses until both he and Luna became aware of the bodies shifting noisily in the pews. Clearing his throat loudly, his eyes revisited the book on the podium before him.

Slipping into the solitude of darkness, Luna sat at the very end of the last pew, nearest the door. She shook as she watched the priest recite various hymns and barely murmured the responses in turn.

"We must repent for all our sins … especially those of the generations before us. Particularly our parents," he said, his eyes landing on hers. "Those sins are like poison, carrying on in the veins of children and grandchildren."

Luna swallowed. The reaction did not escape the priest's notice. His pupils narrowed, but he moved on, switching topics before closing the mass. Luna made it a point to be the first one out of the chapel. Katrin was flushed as she hurried to keep pace.

"Child, my goodness. I am not as young as you," she wheezed. Luna mumbled an apology, feigning a weak stomach as she helped Katrin into the carriage and swiftly followed suit. However, it mattered little how hastily they left. She still felt the priest's eyes searing into her back.

*****

Once back at the estate, Luna worked tirelessly on the duchess' sheets, scalding her fingers in the basin of hot water. Suddenly, the tension of the last few days broke her. She wept silently, letting her tears fall into the water. A feeling of boundless heartache engulfed her. She keeled over further, feeling the tears streaming down her cheeks before taking a plunge into the basin.

"Oh, papa ... what will I do?" She whispered despairingly. Her body heaved with each wave of piercing, lonely sorrow. She choked on her sobs and suddenly felt the urge to run, to be as far away as possible. She pushed herself to hang the last few linens, though her weeping continued. Katrin was busy helping Mirium prepare a nightcap for the king's party and the women were all retired for the evening as far as Luna could tell.

Sneaking out a side door near the well, she ran toward the gardens and then past them, toward the woods behind the servants' stables. Her ears suddenly picked up on two voices, one of them, the distinctly high-pitched tone of the duchess, the other, a low rumble.

Luna paused near the forest's fringe, resting a hand against a tree as she drew in a lungful of sweet, earthy air. The last of her tears had dried, making her cheeks feel stiff. She subconsciously ran her tongue along her lower lip, tasting a salty tang. She leaned forward, straining to hear the voices, which seemed to be floating from the general direction of the king's stables.

"Darling, I know we have not had much time to get acquainted, but it seems as though you have changed over the last several weeks. I hardly recognize the man Duke Nicolai introduced me to five months ago. The man he so adamantly praised, much to Darius' dismay."

"Please, Duchess Rosalind, don't bring Darius' juvenile reactions into this. And please, understand me when I say I have had much on my mind ...," Caedon said, letting the last word trail.

"Is it to do with the king's negotiations?" She asked, a tinge of desperate hope in her voice.

"No, my father has been much more immersed in that business than I. This has a bit more to do with me, with our future," he said unsteadily, cautiously.

"Oh? And what of it?" she said, suddenly defensive.

"Nothing to alarm you Rosalind. It's really rather, well, it's more to do with me clearing some of the cobwebs in my head. Perhaps I will take a few days away from here, on my own," he said, his voice picking up a bit as though he had just discovered the answer to something. "Yes, yes I think that is what I'll do."

"Well, if you feel that is what you need, I will not object," the duchess said, defeat and consternation in every syllable.

"My darling duchess, I will return before you know it, with a much clearer head, mind you," he said, feigning reassurance. Luna read right through it.

As though he suddenly felt her eyes, he turned his head in her direction, peering through the indigo hues of nightfall. She did not stir, though her breath quickened, along with her pulse.

She heard Caedon take the duchess' hand, kiss it lightly and escort her back to the castle. Feeling lightheaded, Luna sat down, leaning her back against the tree trunk as she felt the bumps of its roots beneath her.

Another bout with tears assailed her and she pressed her forehead against her knees, praying the pain would ebb, even if just for a moment. But it seemed to only storm her insides more, causing her skin to begin to boil. She stood up, afraid of what was to come and blindly ran into the woods. After some time and much running, she found herself in a clearing, occupied only by two giant boulders. She walked over to one, feeling nostalgic for days long passed, an innocent, rock-climbing child long faded.

She knew what she had done was dangerous. She hadn't paid the slightest attention to what direction she ran. It didn't matter. Her skin burned and she desperately longed for a cool surface to press against. The rock's algid exterior, smoothed by the elements, felt blissful. Its cool contrast to her skin seemed as though it would sizzle. She closed her eyes and breathed deeply, feeling the entire world drift away.

It was not until she heard a faint chirping that she realized she had fallen asleep and morning was fast approaching. Luna's mind concocted an image of Katrin's perplexed, worried face when she found Luna's bed vacant. She stumbled to her feet, squinting through the bright light of a rising sun. She looked at the massive rocks, trying to recall from which direction she had approached them last night. Pretty sure of herself, she began walking through the trees in front of her, searching the ground and brush for any disturbance caused by her clambering feet the night before. Save for a few cracked twigs, she saw nothing, allowing doubt tinged with panic to invade her mind.

She became aware of her parched throat. It always felt like agonizing sandpaper the day after an emotional squall. As though answering her desperate pleas, Luna suddenly heard splashing in the distance. She followed the sound, recognizing the fluttering of wings as she drew closer to it. She came upon a small pond with several geese bathing in it, which meant two things. Yes, she had at least found a source of water, but this also meant she was nowhere near the king's castle. Overwrought with exhaustion and heat, Luna sat by the edge of the pond and immersed her face into several handfuls of frigid water.

Her stomach grumbled as she looked around the pond, noticing water lilies floating near the edges, framed by long, whispering reeds and wild orchids. Lying back onto the mossy earth floor, Luna closed her eyes, wondering how in the world she would get back to the castle and pondering if she just might die, right here, in this tranquil haven. After all, no one would know where to look for her ... if they even tried.

Feeling her body give into the sun's warm embrace, she felt her consciousness lulling into a land of dreams, the kind so vague, their details are rarely remembered. Perhaps it was her weakened state, or extreme hunger playing tricks on her mind, but her dreams seemed to lift her, suspending her above the ground.

Am I floating? Have I left my body? Was this what it felt like for my father, my mother? Oh, no ... not my mother.

But that thought was banished by a sound Luna could not place, a creaking perhaps. It did not fit in with the resonance of the pond and trees. Straining her ears, she realized she heard footsteps, and felt a slight rocking beneath her raised body.

She must still be dreaming, but wherever her dreams had taken her, she was no longer near the pond. She felt the familiar softness of sheets beneath her bones and caught the faint scent of honey and tea. Feeling a hand press against her temple, she realized, with a bit of disappointment, that she was indeed not dead. Cringing from the hunger cramps slicing into her sides, she opened her eyes, their blurry vision slowly clearing up to lock onto a pair of stormy blue eyes.

Chapter 13

"How –" she began, hushed by a gentle finger against her lips. Gazing around the small cabin room, Luna registered it was once again twilight, and there was a small fire lit near the door. Her forehead scrunched in complete bafflement. Caedon read her expression and began nodding.

"It's a small log cabin, several miles from the king's estate. The queen, before she passed, would use it often as a reprieve, of sorts, from the royal life. She would come here with the king sometimes, or so my father has told me. Then, after she fell ill, the groundskeeper used it. However, I'm afraid it has been vacant for quite some time now. The king has maintained its upkeep, though, perhaps never quite able to part with it altogether."

Caedon suddenly became cognizant of his rambling and flushed ruefully. Luna mused he had not blushed in such a way since being a child. Her hands reflexively flew to her own tepid cheekbones, causing an instant wave of embarrassment for the vision she must be after a night and day wandering in the elements. But Caedon seemed oblivious.

"I came here to ... to," but he let his words dissipate, his eyes lingering on hers before looking to the dusty floorboards. "Let's just say, I drew inspiration from the late queen."

Luna only nodded, for she recalled the words, both spoken and unspoken, Caedon had said to the duchess.

"I thought I had felt ... or rather heard you last night outside, but figured I might have been mistaken," he said, searching her eyes.

Although she did not say one way or another, he nodded and continued.

"Then I arrived here and spotted a body near the pond and ... forgive me, but I almost could not breathe when I realized it was you. You looked – "

It was her finger that hushed him this time. He paused for what felt like an eternity before bringing his hand up to where hers still pressed against his mouth. He gave it a squeeze before releasing it at her side.

Her stomach made a low rumble. The corners of Caedon's mouth pulled up slightly as he repressed a smirk.

"I have some bread and cheese soup made. It's about all I know how to make," he said apologetically, the genuine care in his voice squeezed Luna's heart.

She slowly pushed herself into a seated position while Caedon served her. The potent cheddar aroma made her mouth water. Trying not to inhale the meal, Luna paced herself. She would never admit this to Dirdra, and perhaps it was just the mere fact she was famished, but Caedon's cheese soup tasted better than any she had ever had before.

Though she barely finished, he automatically poured a half bowl more. It seemed to nestle its way into every region of Luna's stomach, satisfying all its demands. Suddenly, Katrin's face popped into her mind.

"Oh no, how will I let Katrin know ..." she began, trailing off as she saw Caedon shake his head.

"I've already sent word to Katrin via the messenger boy. I had previously instructed him to come by here this afternoon in case there was anything else I needed," he said. "I told him to tell her you had felt ill and I found you very weak and dehydrated by the gardens, so I escorted you to the nearest village doctor. I did not get into too much detail, but she knows you are in good hands and just needed a day or two of rest."

Luna was at a loss for words. Why on earth would this man who hardly knew her, was well above her station, not to mention promised to another, continue to go through all this trouble? It was mind-boggling to say the least. It eerily reminded Luna of her mother's note to Duchess Lucinda, who had also apparently come to her aid in some way.

Caedon studied her face, his eyes narrowing when they landed on hers. She smiled, praying he saw the gratitude in them.

"You're welcome," he whispered before rising to add a log to the fire. Though it was summer, the evening brought a slight chill. Caedon grabbed the chair he had placed next to the bed, moved it back near the table and sat down, clearly wanting to give Luna some room – or perhaps needing some himself.

She felt his eyes on her, though her eyes were mesmerized by the fire, its flames dancing and licking the top of the hearth. Caedon followed her gaze, then looked back at her. Though she knew he would never pry, she felt his curiosity and it terrified her. For some strange reason, she trusted this man completely and barely knew him. She briefly wondered if it was a family trait. Perhaps her mother had felt the same with his. The fact they were linked in some way made her body tingle and her fingers go numb.

She pondered how much to say and for once, against her father's dying words, she followed her heart.

"Yesterday, I was mourning my father, among other things, when I felt the strong urge to run, to be away from there. I was not thinking, just doing. I needed a cool surface," Luna said, realizing how ludicrous she must sound and deciding to backtrack her thoughts.

"Sometimes, when my emotions become ... overwhelming, my body reacts in an ... unconventional way, I suppose," she said, choosing her words carefully. "It's nothing alarming, it's often too subtle for most to notice, but I suppose some would say it's ... unnatural."

Luna swallowed, realizing her mouth had run away with her. Caedon never flinched, or let on that he was taken aback, disgusted or even fearful in any way. Either he was a master of facades or he really did not find what she said to be shocking.

"And because of this ... different way that you respond to emotion, you are afraid of people?" he asked, his face continuing to betray nothing.

Luna nodded, scared to say more. Caedon seemed to sense her anxiety and pulled his chair back to the place it was before, only a few feet from her. His mind chewed over a few thoughts before he spoke.

"Has there ever been an instance when you thought perhaps you would hurt someone?"

Luna gulped, her eyes instantly brimming as the haunting memory of the old gypsy stormed her mind.

"Once," she said, but could not say more. Caedon nodded and didn't press further. Luna took that as a positive sign, though she could not be sure yet.

"I have one more question. I promise it does not pertain to any of what we were just discussing. Was it you the other day, in the garden with Darius?"

Luna nodded again, feeling her strength returning. Her raspy voice came out sturdier than before.

"I went out there on my own, to see what it was like. I had never seen something so magnificent in my life. I rested my eyes for a moment and must have fallen asleep. By the time I awoke, it was dusk, and as I started back, Darius stopped me," she said, remembering the threat in his eyes and immediately halting her words.

"Did he do something to you?" Caedon asked, his body suddenly rigid with tension, his voice no longer gentle but carrying an uncharacteristic note of darkness. Luna shook her head but looked down. It was a telling sign only her father knew, though Caedon seemed privy to it as well. He pressed her with his eyes, but she gave him nothing else, and after a few moments, he backed down and just nodded.

So much bubbled and churned under the surface of them both that Luna could hardly breathe. If her intuition was not betraying her, she sensed he was the key to the mystery of her mother's letter. Yet, she was unsure of how to approach it, or if she should altogether. It had been ingrained in her mind to trust no one, yet nothing her parents ever said prepared her for the petrifying, almost uncontrollable pull she had to this man.

"You know ... I see that you sometimes fear yourself, but if no one else has told you this before, I would be surprised. You have an amazing way of bringing calm and peace to a person while, at the very same moment, being an incredible spark to a flame," he said, letting down his usual mask of vigilance.

Besides her father and mother, who always saw every piece of her as a gift, this was the first time Luna had ever heard similar sentiments. She found herself unsure how to react. Her eyes, however, never failed her. Though it was not until Caedon extended a handkerchief toward her that she realized she had been crying.

He looked down suddenly, his forehead scrunched as he stared at the cracks in the floorboards. Then he raised his eyes back up to hers.

"I'm sure, if my suspicions are accurate, that you overheard my discourse with the duchess last night," he said, though there was not even the slightest hint of censure or disappointment in his tone. When Luna did not respond, he took it as an affirmation and continued.

"Then you heard me speak of an unclear mind, stress and mottled thoughts," he said. "Well, to be frank, I have found myself in very foreign, very peculiar territory of late. Though you have no clue what I'm speaking of, let us just say many long forgotten, meticulously buried memories and emotions have recently surfaced. I cannot be certain of the exact instant of change, but it seemed to take place the moment I returned a scarf to a very hauntingly beautiful, unsuspecting servant."

Luna caught her breath; her heart seemed to skip several beats.

"You see, your eyes bear a striking resemblance to my late mother's. In fact, for a split second, I thought you were her ghost. But it is not just your eyes, my dear," he said, his voice seeming to melt with each sentiment. "It is your conduct, the way you speak, what you exude in each action you take, in every syllable you utter, in your spirit and your energy."

With every word, he moved subtly closer and Luna remained frozen in place, spellbound by what her ears were hearing. However, just as suddenly as he had melted, Caedon's eyes grew dark and brooding.

"When she ... fell ill and passed," he said, practically forcing each consonant out, "nothing was the same."

Luna sensed the web of implications, but much like her own mother's tale, some secrets were best left alone, at least at the present. The moment passed and Caedon's eyes were once again iridescent.

"Suffice it to say, I wanted to come out here to ... well, so that I could clear you from my mind and any other part of me you seem to have unintentionally invaded," he said, smirking to lighten his words. Luna returned the meager smile. "But as fate would have it, here you are."

At this, his face grew solemn, a fierce intensity following. He moved a few inches closer, leaving very little space between them. Luna felt a strange warmth flood her insides, just beneath her abdomen and below her collarbones. Her skin grew warm, radiating a heat that enveloped Caedon's senses. He sucked in a deep breath. The pause seemed like a millennium, yet before she could exhale, he dove into her lips. Her entire body flushed, breaking out into a sheen lit by the firelight.

His tongue explored every region of her mouth, twirling with hers before pulling back and allowing his lips to move fluidly against her own. She felt him oblivious to reality and she quickly followed in his wake. His hand wrapped around her torso, pressing against her spine and sliding its way up, under her hair to the nape of her neck. Goosebumps spread across her body as his hand dug into her hair, pulling her head firmly against his mouth.

The battle of resistance was lost ... at least this time.

Chapter 14

Luna felt Caedon's hand gently pressing against the back of her head, but was even more aware of the rest of her body only inches from his. As though reading her thoughts, Caedon brought his other hand around her waist to the small of her back and closed the space between them. It felt as though she melted into him, her intense body heat causing a short pause of surprise from Caedon, though he recovered quickly.

As she softened the kiss, she heard a small groan escape his throat. Something raw seemed to burst inside her. Her arms flew to his neck and upper back, pulling him out of the chair and onto the bed as they reclined. Once her head hit the pillow, Caedon finally broke the kiss, breathing heavily against her lips. He pulled his head back slightly and found her moody, silvery gray eyes.

"So this was what you were referring to," he stated rather than asked. His right hand reached up and wiped away the faint sheen on her forehead.

"If you hadn't told me, I would think you dying of fever," he said, his fingers cradling the side of her face and jawline. She slightly shook her head, a rueful smile emerging.

Feeling as though she would burst into flames, Luna began subconsciously untying her bodice. Caedon kept his eyes locked on hers, but moved back slightly as she undid the stiff material and pulled it off, leaving her eggshell peasant top plastered against her sweltering skin. Though Caedon's eyes remained on hers, he was increasingly aware of her state. He, too, began undressing, leaving himself in the same manner he was when Luna first met him. A deep blush spread across her cheeks and neck. Caedon's mouth slightly curved into a smile before growing intent once more.

"Luna ... I – " She halted his words with her lips as he crashed into her. His hands moved along every inch of her body, feeling every curve while hers explored his back, spine, ribcage and shoulders.

She tugged the fabric of his undershirt upward and over his head, leaving his upper body bare. Luna's breath caught at the beauty of his curved shoulders, jutting collarbones and smooth skin.

Suddenly very abashed, she lowered her lashes. Caedon's hand touched under her chin and lifted her head to meet his eyes. The layers of emotion she saw in those abyssal pools of indigo made her eyes glisten. He misread her brimming eyes, his brow furrowing as he backed up slightly. Luna shook her head and swallowed, trying to find her voice.

"It's just ... I've never seen ...," suddenly she was embarrassed by her reaction, though Caedon seemed quite amused. He lay down next to her, pulling her entire upper half into his arms while bringing her forehead against his swollen lips. He kissed her temple, making his way to her ear.

"She was right ... my mother," he whispered, his low voice rumbling against her eardrum. The reference caught Luna's attention, causing her to pull back and look into his eyes, hoping for elaboration. "She told me I would meet you, well ... that I would meet a woman one day who reminded me of her."

"Our mothers knew one another," Luna blurted. Caedon's forehead scrunched as he shook his head in disbelief.

"How do you know this?" he asked, his eyes blazing with interest.

"Duchess Lucinda ... your mother, she corresponded through letters with my mother. One of our servants happened upon one once that was addressed to your mother," Luna said. "I believe they met in person at least once, maybe more, though the letter was almost purposefully vague."

Caedon hung on every word, waiting for her to continue.

"She thanked her for meeting with her and for keeping things quiet between them," she said, squinting as she tried to remember what Regan had told her. "She also said she feared it would be the last time they spoke, yet their bond would remain. My mother was ... she died not long after."

Caedon's expression morphed from raw sympathy to deep concentration, trying to make sense of Luna's words. She was petrified of what she'd already revealed, but it was as though a dam had broken inside her and she was powerless to stop it.

"My mother also told me I would meet someone one day. She did not tell me it was a man, though she said my soul was tied to another's and she was unsure of its outcome … *this time*," Luna said, shivering from the memory of the nightmare. Though she feared Caedon would think her mentally unstable, he remained a mask of pondering, which put her slightly at ease.

"You know, it is against the church to speak of such things," Caedon said. His words held no menace or threat but rather sounded recited. "What was your mother's name?"

"Cybele," Luna said, forcing the name out quickly. Caedon searched his memory, yet came up empty.

"It does not sound familiar, however, I find it very peculiar indeed that your mother would express such similar sentiments as my own," he said.

Luna's eyes begged Caedon to continue.

"My mother always had a way of … knowing things. My father did his best to ignore her, to make her feel guilty, as though she were partaking in the Devil's work," he said, his eyes stormy with emotion. "She was never to speak of it, though she would tell me often of her 'feelings.' Sometimes, she would touch on what my father called the 'blasphemous' idea of the soul having more than one journey on this earth. It disgusted him and frightened my brother. However, I was always fascinated. Though, sometimes she would talk about lifetimes past, how they tie into the present and future, and then her eyes would lock onto mine and an immense sadness would wash over them. It's eerie, how similar it was to the sentiments expressed by Cybele."

Her mother's name on his lips caused another chill to roll down Luna's spine.

"Darius, however, wanted so much the respect of my father, he began believing my mother was evil and my father did nothing to discourage those notions. It's strange, but Darius, even as a young child, was always on his own, always detached on some level. It was as though he rarely felt any human emotion beyond a surface level. My mother never let on, but it was clear in her actions she was aware of this and never quite knew how to reach him. He began to begrudge her, and that blackened seed only grew, nourished by my father's negligence and projections."

Luna's throat became prickly as she attempted a painful swallow. She was terrified of Caedon's next words, however, they never came. He seemed to shut down right in front of her, a shell she could barely recognize. Her hand rose to his cheek, lightly grazing his skin as he looked straight through her.

She pulled him close, his head falling against her chest, over her heart. Its palindrome rhythm seemed to pull him from his dark trance and his arms wrapped tightly around her, as though he were afraid she'd disappear. They laid there in silence, though many thoughts swam through Luna's mind.

Did the nefarious depths I saw in Darius' eyes stem from something that happened with their mother? Did Caedon see right through my carefully painted mask about my own mother?

Yet none of it seemed to matter now. Caedon slid his body up so his eyes were even with Luna's. Turning sideways and propping his head up with his left arm, Caedon gingerly moved a long tendril of hair from her eyes, lingering near her temple. He leaned in, kissing her softly, slowly. She closed her eyes, feeling the pull of sleep on her body, the last of her energy expended by his kisses.

"Let's sleep now. We do not need all the answers tonight," he said against her lips, before letting his head fall onto the pillow, giving in to the night's beckoning slumber.

Chapter 15

The next morning, Luna awoke to the smell of warm curry and bread. The strong spices aroused her senses, pulling her from a hazy dream she was already forgetting. Caedon, however, was nowhere to be found. Luna rubbed her eyes, pulled her disheveled hair back with her scarf and arose from the bed. She walked over to a bucket of water and clean rag, which she wiped her face with before walking over to the curry. Just as she bent down to inhale the rich aroma, Caedon opened the cabin door, a bundle of logs in tow.

Luna reflexively walked over to take them off his hands, but he stopped her mid-stride with his raised hand. He walked over to the hearth and set them down before closing the space between them. His hand came up to her face, framing her cheek while he examined her eyes.

A few minutes later, they ate quietly, both afraid to speak. Finally, Luna couldn't take the silence any longer and looked up from her empty bowl at Caedon's intensely strained expression.

"What will we do?" she finally asked.

Caedon paused, contemplating her words.

"I do not know," he said simply. While Luna was appreciative of his candor, the question remained.

"Something has altered, I fear. Something neither of us has control over," Caedon said. "But I am unsure what to do. I do not know what I *can* do."

Luna looked down then, knowing the meaning behind his words.

"You do not have to do anything. Something may have shifted within us both, but that does not mean we have to continue on in this way," she said, though Caedon already began shaking his head.

"Luna, you don't seem to grasp what I am saying. What has changed inside of me has bound me to you. I cannot escape it. I have a feeling we have known each other before. I don't mean to scare you, or to speak of such 'sacrilegious' ideas, but you haunt me, Luna.

Your soul haunts mine in ways I cannot begin to discern," he said, his trenchant eyes stealing her words.

She could only nod in understanding, for she felt the same inexplicable pull to him. They sat there for a few moments, speaking without uttering a single word.

"I will have to speak with my father when I return, as well as the duchess. Though I had felt general warmth toward her, a sort of friendship and liking, it is quite unfair, indeed, to continue pretending we are enough for each other. It is unjust to have her believing I feel one way when I do not."

Luna watched as Caedon spoke, more to himself than to her. He became aware of this and halted his words.

"But your father wants you to succeed him. It is clear in the way he talks to you, treats you and, of course, in the way he has pushed this courtship," she said.

Caedon nodded in agreement.

"Yes, but my father is not my keeper, Luna. I owe him much, do not misunderstand me, but he has pressured me most of my adult life to find the 'right' person to join hands with and the duchess' wealth is all he cares about. I will deliberate a bit more on the matter, but know that I meant what I said before. I am bound to you now. There is something more to discover. I know you feel it, too. And I fear it is irreversible."

Once again, Luna only nodded, knowing the gesture was enough for him to know she was of the same mind. After today, she knew they both had to return to the castle, not only to prevent further speculation, but because they were both tired of running away from their troubles.

*****

The day passed quickly, as both Luna and Caedon revealed more and more of their dark pasts and the lasting scars their mothers left. Caedon seemed entranced by Luna's tale of how her parents first met. Her mother, a poor gypsy dancing for just enough food to get her and her family to the next village, somehow captured the eye of Luna's father, Jevan, as he passed through the village. Many friends and relatives opposed the union, calling her mother a heathen or a pauper, while her father, though a commoner, owned land and was well-respected in the village. Luna briefly touched on how after her parents had her, the village seemed to quiet down, though there was always an underlying misgiving.

Caedon talked more about Darius, why they were never really close, Darius' envy and the sad tragedy of losing their mother at such a young age. However, Luna saw something much darker in Caedon's eyes when he spoke of her death. It was the same shadow that cast over her own eyes when she mentioned her mother dying, though neither one of them revealed too many details.

Finally, dusk came and went, cloaking them in the night's ashy hues. Caedon lit a fire and a few candles before pulling his chair next to the bed. Luna smiled and shoved it away, moving over on the bed.

"Luna, last night was … I should never have − " but Luna stopped him by raising her hand.

"I know you are trying to be noble and respectful, but I know, intrinsically, you would never harm me and that your intentions are nothing to fear. So please, lie down and go to sleep like a perfectly normal human being. We have enough room and there's nothing logical about you sitting stiffly, upright in a chair."

This seemed to satisfy Caedon, though he was careful not to look at Luna's body, which was only covered by a long, thin cotton blouse. She, as well, made it a point not to look at the outline of Caedon's body as he slipped under the covers. Luna stared at the ceiling, counting the seconds until her heart stopped racing and her mind slowed down. Caedon's back was to her, though she was quite certain he was not sleeping.

She could picture his shimmering eyes, staring at the low-lit fire. Finally, after what seemed like ages, he turned toward her, though she kept her eyes fixed on the ceiling. His energy made her skin tingle, almost to the point of pain. She kept her breathing even, though her heartbeat betrayed her. Caedon continued to stare at her until she finally brought herself to look at him. What she saw, she did not expect. His eyes were filled with tears, though he was trying very hard to keep them at bay.

Luna's hand instinctively flew up to his cheek as she tenderly caressed the skin under his eye with her thumb. A single tear cascaded down his cheekbone. Luna leaned in and kissed the salty liquid while Caedon simultaneously brought his hand up to grasp hers. He pulled back and looked at her, caught off guard by her tender gesture. His eyes were softer than she had ever seen – likely than anyone had ever seen. Just as she was protective of her own emotions, this was a part of Caedon he took care to keep hidden.

Luna did not dare compromise this display of emotion. She assumed it pertained to their earlier discussions, memories of both happy and forlorn pasts. However, the more they looked at each other, the more she realized his tears were for her, for them both. They were mixed with anguish, torment, as well as immense concern. She would not allow herself to believe there was more than deep caring there. That would be impossible.

Caedon watched Luna's eyes intently, as if reading her thoughts, witnessing them war with one another. Finally, he leaned over and pressed his warm lips against her cheek, grazing them over the corner of her mouth until she turned into them. She welcomed his tongue, letting it explore her mouth and move against her own.

Luna's skin glowed in the firelight. Being this close to her, Caedon seemed to grow feverish. He wiped his brow while his chest rose and fell with each breath. Luna pulled her blouse off, careful to keep the sheet pulled up to her collarbones. Though his eyes burned into hers, he briefly let them graze over her body, seeing the faint outline of her breasts through the thin cotton sheets. His breathing quickened as Luna blushingly watched his reaction. This response seemed to melt, yet arouse him further.

He pressed his lips against her neck, moving along her skin while paying particular attention to her collarbones. Bringing his hands to her ribcage, he pulled her upper body toward his lips, pressing them against her nipple, taut beneath the sheet. Luna let out a soft moan, feeling the heat from his mouth through the cotton. It ignited her body while causing a heat to rise from her inner thighs. She began to tremble slightly.

His mouth gently nibbled around her other nipple, wetting the sinuous cloth with his tongue. As he made his way to her waist, he felt her abdomen tighten beneath the fabric. Every curve was accented as his mouth dipped across her navel. Luna let out a roused sigh as her fingers found his hair and gently tangled through it. Caedon felt the heat of her body against his face as he kissed along her waistline, grazing his teeth along the sheet against her hipbones and causing her to arch backward. Caedon caught his breath as he looked up the length of her. Her ribcage slightly jutted out, her graceful neck arched as her head drew backward.

Her scent permeated his senses, bringing his mouth back to her waist and sweltering body. With each kiss came another moan and a powerful wave of heat that felt as though it would burn his skin off. He winced, though the sensation felt torturously good. As his mouth and tongue burrowed deeper and lower, Luna's body began to pulse beneath his arms. Her fingers pulled a bit tighter against his hair as he felt her body convulse slowly, then tense up and finally, she arched back, breathed deeply and paused.

It was as though the moment froze in time. Caedon's mouth pressed into her, his brow furrowed as he looked up at her eyes. Astonished, he saw flames framed by ebony irises mirrored back at him.

And just like that, the moment broke.

She released, letting out soft whimpers as each wave rolled through her body. Caedon slid back up to her face, wrapping his arms around her searing skin. She quivered inside his embrace, as a fine sweat beaded on her forehead, along her temples and above her swollen upper lip. Caedon brushed it away with the edge of the sheets as Luna looked into his eyes – hers no longer fiery, but silvery gray and filled with tears.

Caedon's mouth turned down slightly, unsure of her emotions, but Luna already began to shake her head, stalling his thoughts. It was then he realized the tears were born of deep, blissful joy and the moment was to be cherished.

Though his body ached with longing, pressing hard against the length of her soft skin, he reached to the deepest regions of his mind to find control. As her trembles subsided, Caedon's sharp yearning lost a few of its thorns, leaving his body strangely at ease and profoundly calm.

Feeling like creatures born in a new light, they held onto one another, afraid of what the outside world would bring.

Chapter 16

The incessant chirping of robins pierced Luna's dreams, causing her to groan while stretching her stiff muscles. For a moment, she thought she was back home in the village, but when she felt a body stir next to her, the previous night's events invaded her mind. A blush spread across her face and neck. She heard a small amused exhale and looked to her right and into the eyes of an alert Caedon, who apparently had been awake for some time.

"Are you hungry?" he asked, studying her face and eyes. She nodded, hearing her stomach growl, which drew a soft smile from him. He got up, still half-clothed and Luna examined his beautiful frame, muscular legs and curved back. When he turned around with buttered bread in hand, he stopped mid-stride at Luna's awed expression. It was Caedon's turn to blush, making her grin in return.

Once their appetites were satisfied, they looked at each another and nodded. It was time to head back to the castle … and an uncertain reality. Libra, in all his sterling glory, stood near the cabin, tied to a tree. Just before Caedon leaned down to offer a lift, he brought his hand under Luna's chin and pulled her face up toward the sun. Its rays glistened through the vast oak trees, causing the shadows of their leaves to dance upon her face.

"You know … Libra is almost the same color as your eyes right now," he whispered, his tone heartbreakingly soft. Luna moved into him, hovering near his lips, her lowered lashes glistening under the golden hues of the sunlight. Caedon stared for a moment, then lowered his head to meet her lips. The kiss was soft, yet hungry, and both of them continued it far longer than intended.

Caedon helped Luna onto the horse and followed suit. His body pressed into her back, causing a rush of blood to her face. Grabbing the reins, Caedon's arms squeezed her sides as he commanded Libra's powerful legs forward.

The journey was quiet save for the cracking branches and caked dirt beneath the stallion's hooves. Caedon and Luna did not dare disturb the silence. There was nothing either could say to make the day ahead easier. Once the king's stables were in sight, Luna's stomach cringed. Caedon felt the tension and brought his lips to her ear.

"It will be okay," he said in a gravelly whisper that both elated and calmed her.

While the dark shadow inside her told her differently, she chose to ignore it ... today. Its foreboding message would plague her tomorrow. Just before the edge of the forest, Caedon pulled Libra to a halt. The horse shook his head and snorted in frustration. Caedon got down and extended his arms to Luna. She slid down into them easily, allowing him to carry the full weight of her for a few moments. He did so easily and held her up slightly longer than necessary before planting her feet on the supple earth.

She inhaled the sweet air, closing her eyes to the tranquil, potent aroma of lush grass and moss mixed with the damp bark of surrounding trees. Squinting through the sunlight, Luna found Caedon's eyes. They had previously decided to part ways and arrive separately. Luna knew Katrin would have been discrete with the staff about Luna's whereabouts and the nobles would never have noticed her absence, save for, perhaps, Darius.

Pulling her from such anxious thoughts, Caedon gently grabbed the back of her head and brought her briskly in for a kiss. His lips eagerly crashed into hers and she gladly parted her own to feel the tenderness of his tongue. Her hand flew up to the back of his head and pulled him harder against her. He responded with a soft, deep groan. She softened the kiss, slowing her lips down, then applied more pressure, nibbling on his lower lip and eliciting another moan. The kiss ended in a languid, sensual dance, as they both hesitantly pulled back, lingering for a few moments.

Luna saw something in Caedon's gaze that brought both elation and terror to her bones. It was a depth of emotion that pierced through her heart. Caedon's vulnerable expression registered what she saw and felt. He looked deeper, fervently searching her eyes for emotion. Luna felt powerless to stop him.

After several excruciating seconds, his eyes suddenly softened and his hard, chiseled jawline relaxed. He backed up toward Libra, releasing his arms from Luna's body, though letting his fingers linger on her chin.

They both nodded briskly at one another and Luna gathered her skirt and began walking toward the servants' wing. Caedon would wait a few moments and then escort Libra to his stall in the opposite direction.

Once Luna made it to the servants' side entrance, she stopped and took a few deep breaths to collect herself before pushing the bulky, wooden door open. A wave of heat washed over her as she spotted Mirium near the oven. Luna tiptoed to the corridor, hoping to get to her room before encountering anyone. However, Katrin was pushing a cart of blankets toward the lift when she spotted her.

"Well aren't you a sight for sore eyes," she exclaimed, abandoning her cart and hustling in her awkward gait toward Luna. She immediately gave her a tight embrace. The display of affection from Katrin took Luna off guard, though she quickly returned the hug and smiled.

"What did the doctor say? Are you alright? Did the rest help?"

Luna laughed, thinking of Caedon as her "doctor," and flushed a deep rose color. Katrin's face turned worried, misreading her reaction for stress. Luna placed her hand heavily on Katrin's shoulder and looked in her eyes.

"I am fine. I pushed myself too hard, was under-nourished and sleep deprived. That is all. It is only a matter of me taking better care of myself," Luna said, making sure Katrin showed signs of comprehension rather than worriment or suspicion.

This answer and explanation seemed to suffice and besides telling Luna to take it easy the rest of the day, Katrin went back to her task and Luna to her room, where she had a warm bath.

*****

The next morning, Luna went to the well to grab several buckets of water for Mirium when she overheard voices near the front gate. Chalking up the chatter to the guards, Luna ignored it, until she heard the familiar drone of Darius' voice. She moved near the stonewalls of the servants' wing, where she could get a bit closer yet remain out of sight. She could not make out the words, but her heart dropped the moment she peeked around the wall and spotted the magistrate from her village. It seemed he and Darius were old friends, talking lightly, chuckling and jesting with each another.

Luna eased her mind a bit. Though it was clear they were comfortable with each other, she convinced herself it was not a cause for worry, shut her mind off and walked back to the well. She was quite startled when she saw Duchess Rosalind standing next to it, staring at her.

"Your Graciousness, is something the matter?" Luna asked, immediately bowing her head and avoiding the duchess' eyes for fear of revealing everything with her own.

"Were you eavesdropping?" she asked, her tone lightly amused but laced with tension.

"Yes. I was," she said, straightening up and finally meeting the duchess' eyes. She knew the laws of karma all too well and lying would do no good.

The duchess' lips parted, surprised by Luna's candid response.

"Well, at least you are honest about it. I heard you were sick."

It was Luna's turn to open her mouth in surprise. Why on earth would it matter to any of the royals if she were dead, let alone sick? Briefly studying the duchess' eyes, she realized it did not matter to the rest of the party. But it sure seemed to matter to her. Luna was baffled by who told her, knowing Caedon would not offer such information.

"I noticed you were not helping the older woman you usually work with, so I asked her," the duchess said, answering Luna's unspoken question.

"So, you were ill ... for the past couple of days," she said, gauging Luna's reaction. Keeping her hands at her sides, Luna only nodded. The duchess, in all her glowing beauty, studied her before deciding she was done with the conversation. She swiftly gathered her skirts and walked toward the gardens. Luna watched her graceful retreat briefly before turning back to the well.

She did not know for sure, but she assumed Caedon had not yet decided or expressed anything definitive to the duchess, though she could be certain he was avoiding her. Luna shook her head and squeezed her eyes tightly shut, momentarily wishing the last few days had never happened.

And then suddenly, her eyes flew open and over to the stables before she even realized Caedon was there. Her heart began pounding in her ears. As if sensing its thrumming pulse, he looked over at her, catching her eye. She watched as his stressed, severe expression morphed to one of tranquility. The corners of his mouth turned slightly up just as they both sensed Duchess Rosalind's eyes.

Luna quickly looked down, grabbing two buckets of water and hastily making her way to the door, while Caedon met the duchess' probing glare. She glanced at the door where Luna entered, then back at Caedon. Slightly shaking her head, as though ridding herself of a bad dream, the duchess softened her face and greeted him.

Meanwhile, Darius – who had dismissed the magistrate moments earlier – stood in the shadows, watching the brief exchange while rubbing his fingers over a scrap of fabric, torn from a piece of clothing he was quite sure belonged to a certain raven-haired servant.

Chapter 17

Luna feigned lightheadedness the following Sunday to evade mass and the threatening recognition in the priest's eyes. She realized both the king's party, as well as most of the servants, were away for the morning, so she could enjoy the solitude. Knowing she had to be careful where she went because of her faux ailment, Luna decided she would risk a walk to the king's stables to see Libra.

She grabbed a bucket of feed to take with her, giving her a reason to go in case someone noticed. As soon as she set foot in the barn, her nose was overcome with the powerful scent of horsehide, straw, damp dirt and leather riding saddles. She walked over to Libra, who, as if sensing her arrival, had his head sticking out over the stall door waiting for her touch.

She stretched out a handful of feed toward his giant snout. He sniffed her – his hot breath feeling wonderful against her cold hand – before nibbling from her open palm. Luna giggled a bit, tickled by his nose, and set the bucket on his side of the stall for him to eat from at his leisure. She heard a deep creaking sound near the door and whipped her head around to a dark silhouette lurking in the shadows.

"Hello?" she said, her voice low and steady, despite her heart jumping into her throat.

The form moved into the light, revealing a smirking Darius. Luna swallowed hard and moved her body slightly back, closer to Libra, who merely looked up at Darius and snorted, then buried his nose back into the bucket.

"How are you feeling today ... Luna? You didn't attend mass I see," he said, continuing to walk toward her slowly. She decided fear was what Darius thrived on and she would not give him the satisfaction.

"I'm better, but still felt a bit woozy this morning, so I chose to stay in. However, I grew restless and decided to come here. The horses calm me," she said, offering up more information than usual, hoping Darius would be distracted.

"So, my chivalrous brother came to the rescue again, I hear. What doctor did he take you to?" Darius asked, though it was clear in his sarcastic tone he believed none of it. Luna contemplated her next words, but chose silence instead. She glared at him, her eyes narrowing with every step he took. She remained calm, taking deep, even breaths.

Finally, Darius stopped, though he was only a few feet away.

"What do you want?" she asked, her tone wary.

He studied her a few moments, then pulled out a metal flask from the inside flap of his vest. He twisted the top open, took a swig, then offered the bottle to her. She shook her head tersely, gritting her teeth. He smiled at the noticeable flex in her jaw.

"I find that this calms me much more than a horse," he said, moving closer. The stench of brandy on his breath made Luna's stomach curl as she turned her head away.

"Well, I'm afraid my endearing brother will not be making an inopportune entrance this time," Darius said, closing in on her. Luna moved backward, coming up against the corner of the stall door and barn wall. Darius blocked her in.

"I realize now, all Caedon wanted was to have what I had set my eyes on first," he said, looking the length of her. Luna's hands slowly rolled into fists at her sides.

"You see, it is not some petty spat over a female. Most times, Caedon's taste in women, when he displays any, is quite different from my own ... until now. I knew you were not just some mundane servant girl. I knew it and then Caedon caught wind of my discovery."

"And what ... discovery is that?" Luna asked, her voice raspy but steady.

"I knew she would find a way to haunt me, I just did not realize it would be through the eyes of some pauper gypsy girl," Darius said, seemingly more to himself than Luna. "Then again, it seems quite fitting she might have sent you as a final curse from the grave ...

you with your dark hair, your evocative eyes, your enticing scent. Everything about you screams temptation and heresy."

She rattled her brain, trying to figure out the meaning behind his words and his crazed eyes, but came up empty. Did he mean some past love, perhaps unrequited ... or was he speaking of Lucinda? Luna could not afford to betray anything, so she continued to stare back at his ebony irises with her own blackening eyes.

It was clear the alcohol had some influence on his thoughts and actions, but it was merely a catalyst for what was always lurking in the deepest regions of his conscience.

"But you are different, somehow. You are unlike her in that way. I just cannot put my finger on it, well ... figuratively anyway," he said, taking his hand and grazing it along the side of Luna's jawline. She flinched at the touch but said nothing, hoping she could contain herself.

Darius brought his lips to her neck, kissing the length of it to her collarbone. She closed her eyes tight and attempted to control her breathing. Her hands curled and uncurled at her sides while Libra began twitching his tail nervously and scraping his hoof against the stall floor.

Darius, completely engrossed in Luna's skin, noticed none of this. His eyes slithered up her neck and locked onto hers. They seemed entranced somehow, almost lost. This frightened Luna more than his usual menacing glare. She pushed him back, but he held himself in place, barreling his chest back toward her until he crushed her against the wall.

Libra grew more agitated and began whinnying while an oblivious Darius bit into Luna's shoulder, not quite hard enough to draw blood, but painfully nonetheless. Luna grimaced but kept all sound from vacating her throat, not daring to give him the satisfaction. His hand went to her knee and slid up under her skirt to her inner thigh. She instinctively locked her legs together, blocking his hand from getting higher.

"Stop. Please stop," she whispered, shaking not from fear, but from the strain of controlling her temper and her body, which felt like it could burst into flames at any moment. Darius ignored her pleas, shaking his head mockingly.

"Your body seems to be telling me otherwise," he sneered, fighting against her strength. In one quick motion, he thrust his hand upward, sending a jolt of searing pain throughout Luna's body. She heaved backward, hitting her head hard against the wall. Libra let out a snort before ramming a hoof into the stall door. Darius flinched at the sound, but stared in complete amazement at Luna's face.

"You are boiling!" he exclaimed, fighting the pain in his hand. "It is almost as though you are searing the skin right off my hand."

"Help me, somebody!" Luna screamed, losing her restraint.

Darius took his free hand and ripped her blouse, exposing her left breast. He inhaled sharply as his lips began to quiver in anticipation. He brought his mouth to her nipple and bit down hard, drawing blood. Luna cried out in anguish as she grabbed a handful of his hair and tugged as hard as she could. Darius' head whipped backward with the motion, bringing his eyes level with hers. They were crazed, nebulous. Luna slammed a fist into his cheekbone, jerking his head sideways. He slowly turned it back toward her, his lips spreading into a malevolent grin.

"Sto –" she began before Darius crushed her mouth with his own, muffling her cries.

She kneed him in the pelvis, but he didn't react the way she had hoped. Instead, it seemed to rile him more. He put his hand around her neck and began squeezing. Luna gasped and choked from the pressure on her esophagus. Struggling against him, she felt Libra become more restless beside her. She stifled another yelp through watery eyes.

Then her attention flew past Darius' head at the opposing window where she heard a shuffle. She caught a glimpse of long flaxen hair before it disappeared.

Enraged, she looked into Darius' eyes, her body trembling in pain that felt like a thousand bee stings. Her eyes grew as dark as onyx. Momentarily startled, Darius withdrew his hands and released her body as he backed a few inches away. Luna caught a glimpse of an old fear triggered in Darius as he tried to hide his eyes by looking down at her legs.

It was then Luna felt something wet trickle down her thigh. She looked down to see a dark, crimson liquid. His forceful hand had caused her to bleed. Her body broke out in a sweat as she looked up into Darius' aroused eyes, instantly bringing all thoughts to a halt. He swallowed, his Adam's apple rising and falling to the rhythm of Libra's fidgety breaths.

Everything suddenly seemed to stop, as if all three of them were suspended in time. Then Darius made the mistake of moving slightly forward. The stall door flew open, knocking him backward and then to the ground. Luna gasped in shock as she stared at the towering silver stallion. Darius shook his head, which had hit hard against the opposite stall door, and scrambled to his feet. Clearly rattled by the impact, he looked at Libra as though noticing him for the first time, his eyes wide in surprise.

"That horse looks positively mad!" he yelled, causing Luna, now shielded by the opened stall door, to look into Libra's eyes. Indeed, they showed a wild glint. The horse rose up on its hind legs, letting out a whinny so shrill, Luna's hands flew to her ears. When he came down, he threw his large head back, then brought his front leg up before slamming it down hard against the ground and scraping it backward. Darius looked to Luna then, realizing Libra's sights were only on him. His eyes opened in realization.

"You are doing this! It's the Devil's work!" he cried out before taking off toward the stable doors.

Luna stood completely still, slowing down her breathing while keeping a cautious eye on Libra, who immediately calmed down the moment Darius exited. After a few deep breaths and slow exhales, Luna stepped around the stall door to face the glorious beast that had saved her. He nickered quietly as she reached out her hand, palm up, toward his face. He gently breathed into it.

His eyes were soft and innocent once more. She pressed lightly against his chest and he quickly began backing up until she could close the stall door. After securing the latch, Luna covered herself up as best she could and scampered toward the door, desperate to wash her body in scalding water to erase Darius' stench from her skin.

When she opened the door, she was met by a pair of startled blue eyes. Caedon immediately skimmed over her body and saw the tattered state she was in.

"I thought I heard Libra acting up, so I came to see ... " he trailed off as his eyes caught the blood, now dried and caked on Luna's knees and calves.

"Luna! What on earth – "

"I fell," she interrupted. "It was my fault really, my blouse caught on a nail, I was thrown off balance and gashed the inside of my knee on a sharp stone by one of the stalls."

Caedon did not believe a single word, however, as he pulled her into his arms and pressed his cheek against her tousled hair.

"Luna. What are you not telling me? My brother was just found a few minutes ago collapsed on the ground. It appears he suffered a very severe blow to the back of the head and must have fallen unconscious from the rapid swelling."

Luna pulled back at Caedon's words and glared into his searching eyes.

"They're not sure what happened because no one saw him, or at least, no one is claiming to have seen what happened. But from the looks of things here, I can only assume ... "

Luna nodded, tears suddenly brimming her eyes before she collapsed into his arms.

"What did he do to you?" Caedon growled, his voice carrying the same ire Luna's had just moments ago.

"It's nothing, Caedon. Please, please do not tell anyone. I am okay. He did not hurt me too badly," she sobbed against his chest. As each word spilled out, Caedon's arms tightened more around her body, his hands tensing into hard fists.

"What is happening to him now?" she asked, looking up at Caedon through tear-streaked eyes. The innocence he saw in them softened his grip and he pulled back a bit.

"King Bertrem's personal physician is assisting him, but he said it may take him a few days to recover before he wakes up. He could suffer some minor memory loss, which could work in our favor," Caedon said, his voice now calm and collected. Luna nodded, graciously taking the handkerchief he offered to dry her eyes.

"We should get you taken care of as well," he said, already leaning down to pick her up. But Luna stopped him and lifted his chin to look into her eyes.

"I will be okay. I promise. I just need a warm bath. It looks far worse than it is," she said. Caedon still held onto her as they made their way to the well. Luckily, everyone seemed so preoccupied by Darius, there was not a soul in sight. Once by the well, Luna stopped Caedon and assured him she was well enough to get inside on her own.

As he began hesitantly walking away, she grabbed his shoulder and gently pulled his ear down to her lips.

"Please give Libra a kiss for me."

Chapter 18

It had been a little more than three days and Luna's nerves continued their violent dance while she waited for news about Darius. Katrin did not show any signs of suspicion at Luna's inquiry, but she tended to know more than she let on. Regardless, Luna explained that she had witnessed several members of the staff carrying Darius after his collapse and was curious.

After hearing no news, she prepared her horse and cart for the village, hastily shortening the reins and hopping in. She approached the manor to find Dirdra and Regan pulling a few weeds by the stone path to the door. They heard the cart come to a halt and slowly rose from their kneeling positions. Luna saw tension in both of their strained smiles and knew something was wrong.

As she walked over to Regan, Luna searched her eyes for answers but found fear instead.

"What is it?" she asked.

Dirdra spoke before Regan could answer.

"Let us go inside and talk."

They led the way and Luna followed silently. Once inside, Dirdra gave Luna a cup of tea and some biscuits before settling down at the kitchen table alongside a solemn Regan.

"We had an unexpected visit from a priest this morning," Dirdra said slowly. Luna's stomach knotted immediately, knowing where this was leading. "It was Father –"

"I know who it was," Luna snapped, regretting the harsh bite the moment it left her lips. However, Dirdra was unaffected. "What did he say?"

"He just asked about you, about your background," Dirdra said. "I recognized his name. That's the only way I knew it was ..."

Luna didn't need Dirdra to finish the sentence. All three sat in silence for a few moments before Luna spoke again.

"What did you tell him?"

Dirdra's eyes fell to the table as she nervously fingered the floral napery.

"What could I say? I told him the truth. I mean, I didn't tell him *everything*. I just told him who your father was. I said I did not feel comfortable answering anything else after that, though he pressed about your mother."

Luna swallowed hard and chewed over Dirdra's words. Finally, Regan spoke.

"What should we do?"

"Nothing. At least, not right now," Luna said, contemplating whether she should come forward or not about the recent goings on at the king's estate. She decided against it. The less they knew, the better protected they were.

"Luna? Is there something we should know?" Regan asked, as if reading Luna's mind. Luna looked into her eyes and slowly shook her head. Though Regan knew it was a lie, she left it alone.

"I'm going back to the estate. Perhaps facing him will be better than running," she mumbled, more to herself than anyone else. Dirdra and Regan exchanged worried looks before Luna clasped both their hands across the table.

"It will be okay. I promise. You both will be fine no matter what."

"Luna! Don't you dare talk like that. You sound just like ..." but Dirdra trailed off, her eyes beginning to brim with tears. Luna gave her hand a squeeze.

"It is not the same thing," Luna said, feigning as much reassurance as she could muster, though Regan was not fooled. They rose from the table to hug Luna, then Regan followed her outside to the cart, wrapping herself around Luna's right arm and leaning her head on her shoulder like they did when they were younger. Their sisterly bond always made the neighbors gossip, as did her parents' family-like treatment of all their household staff. At this point, Luna could care less.

"Does any of this have to do with Lucinda?" she whispered. Luna nodded slightly, trying not to give too much away. "Did you find out if they did, indeed, know each other?"

Luna nodded again. Regan understood this was all she would get from Luna and backed off, stepping away after giving her a curt kiss on the cheek. As Luna began her return to the castle, she looked back, watching Regan's waving hand recede into the distance. A sigh escaped her lungs, causing the horse to neigh softly.

*****

It was dawn, the sun barely peeking over the horizon, but Luna was wide-awake, soaked in sweat from frayed nerves and sour fear. She immersed herself in a bath to relax before mass and then prepared the carriage to take her and Katrin to the chapel.

This time, Luna walked in calmly, holding her head up and meeting the priest's expectant eyes with courage. He seemed taken aback by her bold demeanor, but proceeded with the homily as naturally as any other Sunday.

Once mass was over, Luna told Katrin she wished to stay after and speak with the priest alone, for a confession. Katrin said she would send someone for Luna shortly, but Luna turned down the offer, explaining the fresh air and exercise would do her some good. Though Katrin was hesitant, mentioning Luna's recent poor health, Luna convinced her she would be okay.

Once alone, Luna walked down the center aisle toward Father Geirnuk, who looked as though he were expecting her. She lowered her eyes to the ground and knelt down before him, adhering to religious decorum. This gesture seemed to shock the priest. He did not say anything at first, just stared down at her for a few moments.

"What is it you wish to confess, my child," he said, clearing his throat uncomfortably. Luna kept her eyes fixed on the priest's black, cracked shoes. After several more moments of silence, she felt a hand reach down and catch the bottom of her chin, lifting her head to look up.

Her silvery eyes caught the priest's eyes, which had darkened to the color of seaweed. He gasped then, as if seeing a ghost. She felt his hand tremble beneath her jaw as his eyes narrowed.

"Who was your mother?" he asked, slowly. Luna stood, bringing her face level with his.

"Why do you ask questions to which you already know the answer," she asked, causing his eyes to narrow further.

"Do not test me child," he said, crossing his arms and squaring his shoulders. Luna lifted her chin slightly higher and continued to stare back. The priest, realizing he was not going to get an answer, stepped closer, hoping to intimidate her. Luna stood her ground, though her stomach began to twist as she noticed the priest's breath deepen.

"Her blood flows through your veins," he said, as though this explained everything. Luna continued to remain expressionless. "Don't you see? I fear I will have to discover whether you are tainted by the Devil as well. It was my intention all those years ago, but you and your father ... mysteriously vanished."

Luna's jaw clenched at the mention of her father and that night, but her face remained void of emotion. Father Geirnuk took another step closer, bringing his face inches from hers. She felt his acrid breath on her skin, but kept her eyes locked on his.

"Even now, your eyes are changing," he said, a mixture of awe, trepidation and disgust in his voice. "Just like *hers* did."

A warm gust of wind blew through the church doors, hitting them both at once and ruffling Luna's skirt and hair. Luna watched in repulsion as the priest's eyes momentarily rolled back as he breathed in her scent. He then refocused his slightly dazed eyes on her. Luna's vapid mask was beginning to falter.

"I will take my leave now," she whispered.

Father Geirnuk swallowed, guilt written over his entire face at whatever thoughts he had been thinking. He quickly backed away, again, as though a naughty child caught in a wayward act.

Luna turned and briskly walked down the aisle and out of the church, afraid her careful façade would break apart at the seams if she stayed any longer. Once outside, she let the breath she'd been holding whoosh from her lungs and made her way to the dirt road leading to the castle. She was even more grateful for the time alone than she anticipated.

However, her peaceful walk would be short-lived.

Chapter 19

As she came upon a pair of strained voices, Luna instinctively slowed her pace and moved to the side of the dirt path. She walked quietly, hoping she could pass by undetected, but as she neared the heated exchange, she picked up on Caedon's beautiful voice, despite the tension in his tone, and felt her heart skip a beat.

She stopped several yards away, trying to stay hidden in the shadows and wait out the argument. The high-pitched cadence of Duchess Rosalind was hard to mistake and Luna subconsciously bit down on her lower lip as their words floated to her ears.

"I do not understand Caedon. What on earth could have caused this alteration?"

Silence countered as Luna held her breath.

"My dear Rosalind, please understand. This has nothing to do with you. You have been more than admirable and gracious. But I would be remiss if I were to continue on with this courtship knowing I could not give everything you deserve," Caedon said, his tenor much calmer than moments before.

"Oh, Caedon," the duchess said, letting out a slightly maddening giggle. "I may be a woman, but I was also raised a duchess. Unlike most frivolous, silly females, I do not need your adorations, your unparalleled love, your soul. Do not misunderstand. It is not that I am adverse to the notion of love, but I think we can mutually agree this would be a very advantageous match for both families. I care for you, greatly. And I believe you care for me. Love will blossom at its own pace."

Her words flowed poetically, causing Luna's stomach to tighten in envy at such a speech. Caedon seemed to mull over her seemingly genuine sentiments while Luna held her breath in wait.

"They may be frivolous and silly, but those notions are very important to me," Caedon said, trailing off into a whisper, though the note of tenderness in each word did not escape Luna's ears.

The duchess carefully regrouped, studying Caedon while deciding her next approach.

"I did not mean to condescend such ideas, my darling, I just meant that … well that I do not *need* those things the way some women do. But that is not to say I am not open to them or do not desire them. We have not even had the chance to let something grow and develop," she said, hesitating for a moment. "Is it … is it possible you do not find me attractive?"

"Of course not," Caedon quickly responded. "You are striking, Duchess Rosalind. And yes, I acknowledge the very obvious benefits of our union, but the things of which I speak are not things that develop over time. They are either there or they are not. Such connections precede us and are only recognized immediately."

Realizing he was treading into hazy territory, Caedon caught himself, knowing he was losing the duchess with every word.

"Your Grace," she said, switching to formality. "My eyes may deceive me. And perhaps Darius is just plain vengeful, but is it possible someone else has caught your eye? Someone … of a *much* lower station?"

Luna sank to the ground, her knees buckling as her skirt flowed out around her. She squinted through the brush concealing her and saw Caedon's jaw flex as his hand slightly clenched at his side.

"Darling," she began, intimate once more. "I do not mean to offend. I once, too, had a crush on a servant boy when I was barely 16. I thought it was a genuinely real emotion. I thought it was love. But of course, my mother showed me just how ridiculous I was being. I realized it was just an infatuation, and after a few weeks, I was able to clear him from my mind and focus on reality once more."

"Duchess Rosalind," Caedon said, faux calm in every syllable. "Do not meddle in that which you are ill-versed. I fear your imagination has run away with you. I appreciate your feelings toward me and I am flattered by the sentiments you expressed earlier, but I will have to stop such tactless insinuations. What I am telling you has nothing to do with my attention being elsewhere. What I am telling you comes from my heart. It is *because* I care for you that I am choosing fairness over insatiability."

The note of caution in his words did not escape the duchess, who had noticeably swallowed her retort. However, she held her ground, bowing gracefully before meeting his eyes again.

"Very well. I will not win this evening. There is no need to continue this discussion right now and I do not need a response, but please think this through a bit more before deciding to break such a pertinent engagement."

While her words expressed slight desperation, she was masterful at keeping any pleading from her tone. Caedon said nothing for a few moments and then gave a brisk nod before extending his arm to escort the duchess back to the castle. When they were beyond earshot, Luna slowly regained her composure and stood back up. She felt guilty for eavesdropping on such an intimate exchange, but she felt more shame for her inadvertent role in it.

As she walked, quiet sobs escaped her throat, sending tears down her cheeks. She had to undo the damage she had done. Somehow, she had to right this wrong, but she was unsure of how to get time alone with Caedon. Then, in an instant, it came to her.

Yes, I know what I could do.

*****

Luna was sure to carry the last load of clean sheets alone. She knocked first, then upon hearing silence, entered the room where she had first encountered those magnetic blue eyes. An unexpected forlorn sigh escaped her before she shook her head and took a step toward the bed. She quickly dressed it with fresh linens before slipping the note she had agonized over all morning between Caedon's pillows, letting a corner peak out far enough to be noticed. She could only hope he would see it before this evening.

Luna finished her chores quickly and headed out to the garden. It was just after sunset and she knew Katrin would begin to worry about her when nightfall approached, but she had to at least see if Caedon would show. Again overwhelmed by multiple fragrances,

Luna grew dizzy and sat down on the same bench she had fallen asleep on previously.

Not long after, she heard soft footsteps on the stone pathway to her right and looked over to find a very strained-looking Caedon. His stature displayed that of composure and guarded nobility, but his haunted eyes showed anguish, longing and warmth. Luna could barely breathe as she quickly stood and bowed, leaving her lashes lowered.

She felt a hand touch beneath her chin, instantly erasing the memory of the last one placed there. Caedon gently pulled her face upward, though she kept her gaze lowered.

"Luna," he whispered, bringing his lips closer to her. She looked up finally, meeting his eyes. They were saturated with concern, causing Luna's heart to melt. How was she going to do this?

"I, I wanted to tell you ... " she trailed off, feeling the warmth emanating from his skin as his eyes penetrated hers. She swallowed, feeling his hand move down her neck to tenderly squeeze her shoulder.

"Are you feeling any better? I kept seeing you, in my mind, the way you looked in the stables. It has haunted me every night this week and I could not, for the life of me, find you to make sure you were okay. Did you have to leave here for a few days?"

His frantic line of questioning took her completely off guard, causing her brow to furrow. Caedon reached up with his other hand to smooth the lines on her forehead as he brought his face closer, studying her eyes.

"I was here. I rested for a day, then I was quite busy, making trips for Mirium to the market and to my village. I am okay," she said, feeling his sweet breath on her lips, causing her heart to race.

"Then what is it? What is wrong?" he asked, his voice hoarse with worry.

"I ... overheard your conversation yesterday. I was on my way back from the church," she said. "I am so sorry, I did not mean to listen, I –"

Caedon silenced her with a sharp head shake.

"I know it was not your intention to overhear, but Luna, nothing I said to the duchess was anything I would not have said to you. In fact, I had planned to do so," he said, taking Luna aback. After a few moments of perplexed silence, she regained her voice.

"The reason I needed to speak with you is ... I fear that I have done something terribly wrong. Your engagement ... I cannot bear the idea that I had –"

Caedon's hand interrupted her, his fingers landing softly on her lips. Luna stared at him in confusion.

"I know what you are thinking. You have no grounds to think it. Yes, something altered the day I met you, but the things that changed were already there, inside me. All you did, all your presence did, was unveil them," he said, applying more pressure to her lips as she started to protest. "There is much more to this story and I believe we should ... no, I believe we must discover the rest."

Luna shook her head in disbelief.

"As for Duchess Rosalind, do not distress yourself. That courtship was always my father's wish, not my own. She is beautiful and gracious, but I know now more than ever she and I will never be happy together, we will never satisfy each another," Caedon said, carefully choosing his words.

"But your father ... " Luna began, as Caedon started shaking his head.

"I will deal with my father. He has been aware of my hesitancy over this union for some time now. I promised the duchess I would give it some more thought, and while I will do so, my heart already knows what my mind will soon catch up to," he said.

Suddenly, sensing their close proximity to each other, both Luna and Caedon backed up an inch, Luna's eyes immediately casting to the ground.

"But you and I ... there cannot be anything. It is not possible," she whispered. Caedon took a step toward her again, bringing his face inches from hers.

"I do not have all the answers and neither do you, but we both cannot deny there is something here. Our mothers knew each other,

Luna. What are the odds of that? Can you deny how you feel, right now, or what you feel?"

Luna swallowed, words failing her. Hearing his breath quicken, she felt hers follow suit. Then, his lips were upon hers, causing a strange jolt of energy to shoot down through her stomach and into her thighs. The kiss was fierce, brief and left her breathless. Caedon's mouth twitched at the corners, suppressing an amused grin.

"How is Darius?" she asked quickly, changing the topic to lessen the flush in her skin. Caedon's eyes clouded over, causing her to instantly regret the change in subject.

"He is still resting but he is conscious. The doctor was right about his memory, though. He does not recall much at all from that ... evening," Caedon said, forcing out the words. "But if he does finally remember, Luna ... for your own protection, you must tell me what happened."

Luna started shaking her head, but Caedon squeezed her shoulders.

"You have to at least tell me something," he said, his grip strong but his voice gentle.

Luna gave him a very pared-down version of the incident, though his own imagination filled in the gaps, causing his hands to become fists.

"He called you evil?" Caedon asked. Luna nodded and his eyes grew darker. "And he said he knew she would return? Did he say who 'she' was?"

Luna shook her head, though she caught Caedon's eyes widening before growing even more ominous.

"I will never make you recall such memories again," he said, his face softening as he cast his eyes over the landscape of her face, jawline and neck. Her heart softened as a tear rolled down her cheek. Caedon wiped it away with his thumb and then brought his lips to hers once again. This time, the kiss was tender and soothing, leaving them both at ease.

"I will not mention a word to Darius or anyone else, and I will try to keep the doctor, as well as my father, from continuing to question him about the incident," Caedon said. "Meanwhile, I will see if I can find out anything more about my mother and her acquaintance with yours. I still have some of her belongings locked away in the chest my father and I always bring on our travels."

Luna nodded, unsure of what to say. They both had dark secrets, but neither was ready to reveal them just yet.

Caedon pulled her into his strong arms, bringing her head against his chest with a gentle hand. She listened to his heartbeat, steadily thrumming against her eardrum.

"And Darius ... he will never touch you again."

Chapter 20

Luna stood outside, letting the wind flow through her cotton blouse and skirt as she stared hypnotically at the moon. Its almost abnormally large presence in the sky caused her to gasp earlier in the night when she had gone to the well for water. Now, it was slightly higher, though it had a blood-red tinge around it, causing her stomach to waver a bit.

Katrin came out a few moments later and stood next to her, casting her eyes upon the natural phenomenon.

"She is quite breathtaking, isn't she?" Katrin asked rhetorically. Luna nodded, keeping her gaze fixed on the crimson sphere. The moon's face seemed to frown at the world below, as if mourning something only the heavens could see.

"Shall we?" Katrin said, looking at Luna's mesmerized, cloudy irises. When she looked at Katrin, the reflection of the burning moon danced like firelight in her eyes, catching the older woman's breath.

Luna quickly looked down and pivoted. The moonbeams washed over her back, spilling across her shoulders and neckline. She extended her arm to interlace with Katrin's and they walked back to the kitchen door.

Gently unweaving her long braids, Luna stood by her bedroom window and suddenly felt a devastating wave of homesickness flood her insides. It brought her to the edge of her bed, where she buried her face in her hands and softly wept.

So many questions, so little time. Luna was more unsure of her future than she'd ever been. Just as her mother had told her, someone she would one day meet would alter her life. But the fear in Cybele's eyes had haunted her.

Though Luna had not understood its meaning then, she recognized it now. Her mother had foreseen Caedon, had witnessed how Luna's soul was tied to his. While she would not dare speak such notions aloud, Luna felt as though she had always known him. It was as if their fates were tied from the moment they met, no ... from even further back than that. Her mother had said she did not know what was to come *this time*.

This time ...

Shaking cobwebs from her head, Luna let out a tear-drenched sigh and gave the forlorn sky a final look before blowing out her candle and slipping under the covers.

*****

The following morning brought with it dispirited news of Lady Beatrice's passing. It would seem she had taken a turn for the worse the previous evening and could not recover. The servants scurried about to prepare a dinner in honor of the lord's wife for that evening.

It had been over a week since Luna met Caedon in the garden. She was a ball of frayed nerves by the time dusk approached and she had to dress the tables in the king's private dining quarters.

The tables were covered in lavish ebony silk cloth, complemented by deep red roses, Luna's favorite kind. Their petals were so dark, they seemed tinted with charcoal hues. Once she lit the candles, Luna went back downstairs. Mirium had asked her if she could lend a hand serving dinner since three staff members had fallen ill two days prior, and it was very hard to refuse since the head cook had promised to compensate with extra wages.

Changing into a long black skirt and bodice, Luna tied her hair back with her mother's scarf. Only Caedon would notice, she realized, smiling. Her stormy, silver eyes stared back at her from the mirror and she shuddered.

Moments later, Luna was standing in the background near the servant door of the king's dining room, waiting alongside Arianna to refill glasses. Mirium had already served the soup and was preparing the main course when the king's personal guards opened the large double doors.

Darius slowly walked in. Luna's stomach sank as she felt Arianna noticeably tense next to her. Luna's eyes flew to a corner table, where she caught Caedon's meaningful glance.

Her eyes then shifted to the duchess – who had ardently watched the brief exchange – before finding solace on Arianna's turgid form. Darius, however, appeared out of sorts as his father briskly made his way to him and led him to the corner table. As they passed, Luna heard the duke whisper in Darius' ear concern about him not being ready to walk, but Darius swatted away his worry.

Arianna began to step forward, sweat beaded on her brow, but Luna stayed her with a gentle hand and nonchalantly grabbed the pitcher of water from her. Once again, Arianna gave her a grateful look before heading to the king's table for refills. As she walked, Luna's suddenly parched throat screamed for the water she held in her hands, but she kept her pace steadfast.

The duchess was busy adding some salt to a bowl of soup for Darius when she looked up to see Luna standing next to her, waiting to fill her glass. She leaned slightly backward, but kept her jade eyes on Luna as she poured. Duchess Rosalind then looked over at Caedon, who was doing his best at avoiding all three of them. Her hand came to rest overtop his as she held Luna's gaze, which did not falter.

"Darius," the duchess said, cutting into the silence. "You remember ... what is your name again?"

Knowing full well the duchess remembered her name, Luna said nothing. However, Darius' attention was caught as he turned to look up at her. His brow furrowed at first, as though trying to place her. Luna quickly looked away and began a hasty retreat, but Duchess Rosalind grabbed her arm at the same time Caedon slipped his from Rosalind's grip, bringing it down on her forearm with a squeeze. The duchess let out a startled gasp as she released Luna and glared at Caedon.

His eyes carried a weighted threat behind them, causing the duchess to collect herself and quickly engage Darius in a fresh topic as Luna made her way back to Arianna.

The rest of the evening passed without incident. Luna practically flew through the servant doors when Mirium dismissed her. However, Arianna grabbed her arm before she made it past the threshold.

"I'm so sorry. Duke Nicolai's son slipped me this paper when I took his plate away. It is addressed to you," she said, a somewhat embarrassed expression on her face. Luna quickly grabbed the note and left. Once within the safe confines of her room, she unfolded the tiny slip and brought it under the warm glow of candlelight.

Dearest Luna, I have found the "trinket" we spoke of the other day. It holds grave discoveries I dare not put down in writing. I'm not sure when or where, but I will find you. ~ Caedon.

Luna read the words over and over again, unable to fathom what he had uncovered. She could not get under the covers of her bed fast enough. It had been a long, irksome day and her eyes, heavy with fatigue, closed barely before her head made it to the pillow.

When she awoke, it was time to help the king's guests into their carriages before they made their way to the funeral service for Lady Beatrice. Luna scurried to meet Katrin and Virgil near the front gates, where she helped a few of the elderly guests walk. Suddenly, she saw a guest she did not anticipate.

Father Geirnuk.

Luna's eyes went wide before she recovered and stepped aside as he walked past her toward his carriage.

"Could you help the duke's son, Luna?" Virgil whispered. Luna looked back to see Darius, using a cane as support. She stood, frozen, but Virgil's rough whisper, repeating himself, shook her from her daze, sending her forward. Darius looked puzzled again as he stared at her, nervously fondling something in his palm. As she approached, her eyes caught the corner of a familiar piece of cloth between his fingers.

Her breath caught, causing Darius' eyes to narrow. He looked down at his hand and then back up to her before his bewildered eyes filled with poisonous recognition. His hand tightened over the scrap of fabric as he took a step backward.

"Don't you touch me," he breathed vehemently before walking

past her. Luna watched as Father Geirnuk studied them both before approaching Darius. Her stomach clenched in terror.

They cannot speak, she thought, panicking, searching for Caedon. But he was nowhere. Nowhere at all.

Chapter 21

Fearing the worst, Luna knew she would not be able to face work. Faking fatigue, she secured a decent window of time to figure out her next move. Everything inside her screamed for her to run but she knew, now more than ever, her past would always find her. It knew no bounds and had even withstood the limits of time.

Luna went to the stables, hoping Caedon would show. He was not with the rest of the funeral party and the words on his note had chilled her to the bone. He must be somewhere close.

Will he find me?

As if hearing her heart's throbbing pleas, Luna heard the sharp creak of the stable door and instantly felt his energy. Her breathing slowed as peace seeped into her veins, bathing her in calmness the moment his cobalt irises met hers.

Forgetting himself, he immediately strode over to her, wrapped his arm around her waist and pulled her body into a strong embrace. She gasped from his intensity.

Pulling back slightly, Caedon brought his hand under her chin and raised her eyes to his.

"My apologies. I did not mean to be so forthright. It is just ... I long for you every hour, every moment I am apart from you," he said through heavy breaths. "I cannot think straight sometimes because of my worry for you. It is as though you haunt every piece of me."

Luna swallowed, taken aback by Caedon's admittance. Save for those few moments in the cabin, she was certain it was the most open he had ever been with anyone and it terrified him.

"Your Grace –" she began.

"Caedon," he softly interjected. She looked down before facing his penetrating gaze once more.

"Caedon," she whispered, "what will we do?"

He stared at her for a few moments more before walking her to a bench near the stable doors.

"Your brother, he recognized me," she said, the words flying out before she could catch them.

"You are certain?" he asked, his eyes narrowing in concentration. Luna nodded, and both looked away, lost in thought.

She felt him turn back toward her, pulling her into another embrace. His soft lips landed warmly on her temple, sending goosebumps across her skin as a soft moan escaped her. The air had a chill, causing her breath to mist as she turned toward him, her eyes sparkling with tears.

"I should tell you ... Father Geirnuk, he knows me. He knows my family, from before," she said. "My mother, she was ..."

But Caedon stopped her with his lips, drawing her into a sensual kiss. His arms wrapped around her, bringing her chest against his. Her tongue twirled around his as she felt his hand slide past the nape of her neck and burrow into her hair. Now, it was his turn to moan.

"Caedon," she murmured against him, slowly pulling back to look into his eyes, "you do not understand, Father Geirnuk condemned my mother and now he has recognized me, as does your brother. They spoke, by the carriage. If Darius told him what happened here with him, I ... I shudder to think what will happen."

Caedon began fervently shaking his head.

"It is nothing. He sustained an injury to his head. The priest knows this. He will consider that when Darius speaks to him. Besides, you do not know that he recalls everything. Maybe he just recalls who you are."

Luna shook her head, remembering the image of foreboding in Darius' face when the realization of her identity dawned on him.

"He remembered."

Caedon searched her eyes before seeing she spoke the truth. He squeezed her hands with one of his, bringing the other up to graze her cheek.

"It will be okay."

Though his words aimed to ease her frayed nerves, they fell hollow against her heart. She knew better, just as her mother had.

"There was something else that happened that night my cart broke down in the woods," Luna whispered, her menacing tears finally making good on their threat to cascade down her cheeks. Caedon pulled out his handkerchief to tenderly wipe them away, but she stayed his hand, wanting his full attention.

"There was a man. An old gypsy. He tried to steal from me. I let him. However, he went after my mother's necklace, which was in a small pouch I had with me."

Caedon's jaw clenched, the muscles noticeably strained against the sunlight pouring through the window.

"It became violent," Luna said, closing her eyes from the memory. "I remember being petrified, then it slowly changed, morphing into a rage I could not control."

Afraid to continue, Luna swallowed and looked down at her lap, feeling the muscles beneath her skirt taut with tension. Caedon patiently waited for her to continue. The next words drifted from her lips in a whisper.

"His eyes became haunted with pain. I believe his heart was giving out on him. But it was not until my hand clamped on his wrist that he screamed in anguish and took his last breath," she said, feeling every word rapidly tumble from her mouth.

Finally, she allowed Caedon to wipe the tears from her skin as he waited for her to meet his tender gaze.

"Luna, it is not humanly possible —"

Her fingers touched his lips as she quickly shook her head.

"Do not tell me it is not possible. We may be condemned to speak of such things, but let us not fool ourselves. We both know there are many experiences we've had in our lives that continue to go unexplained."

Caedon slowly nodded his head, acknowledging her words and accepting their meaning. They were in agreement they could not talk in great detail, but their silence did not chase away the looming reality of the situation.

"There is more," she said, clearing her throat of the swelling lump of anxiety. "When I went home a few weeks after the incident in the woods, one of my servants told me the village magistrate found a piece of cloth on the gypsy that was unexplained since it did not go to anything he was wearing."

Luna waited while Caedon processed her words, then continued when his eyes widened in understanding.

"He did not think much of it because of the gypsy's poor health and homeless condition. However, when I saw your brother on his way to the carriage for Lady Beatrice's funeral, he had that same cloth in his hands," she said, her body trembling. "I am doomed, cursed. I should have left here long ago, when I first caught a glimpse of suspicion. But I stayed, knowing that running would do nothing. That is what my father and I did and look where it got us. He died and left me, to what? To nothing. He knew what was inside of me and he left me anyway. Neither of my parents prepared me for what I am. I do not even know what I am."

Caedon immediately pulled her into his arms, resting his chin on the top of her head. They sat in the deafening silence, pondering her words. She heard a soft whinny from the stall behind them. She did not know the red bay's name, but the mare seemed to watch her with a steady, gentle gaze every time Luna entered the stables. It was as though she knew something – wisdom she was unable to communicate.

A long sigh flowed from Luna's lungs, bringing her body tighter against Caedon's. Responding, he squeezed her, pressing his lips to her ear.

"I am not afraid of you."

His words vibrated against her eardrum, causing warmth to flood her veins. She pulled back and looked into his eyes. Suddenly, she remembered his note and that he had something to tell her.

As if reading her thoughts, he began to shake his head.

"Not here," he said as he stood up, pulling her up with him. "We are going to the cabin. I must hear the story about your mother first."

Terror gripped Luna's heart, but she gave a meager nod, knowing it was time to cross this threshold. She did not understand everything yet, but she felt her mother's presence these past few weeks more than ever before. She had an inkling Caedon was experiencing the same.

Her mind raced at his proposal. How would she explain her absence to Katrin? Caedon squeezed her hand as he let go to prepare Libra for the ride. After a few moments, he tightened the girdle before looking over at her.

"You do not need to tell anyone anything at this point. I have a feeling something very bad will happen the moment the king's party returns, especially if, as you anticipate, my brother spoke with Father Geirnuk and the magistrate. You and I must talk and then I will address my brother. I will have you back by this evening and then I will speak with Darius, my father and the priest. We will make them realize this has all been a huge misunderstanding."

Caedon's rambling betrayed his worry, though Luna already felt something dark brewing in the air. He held out his hand and she took it, deciding to push her doubts aside. After all, the consequences might already be written in the stars.

*****

They rode quickly, neither of them speaking until they spotted the small pond indicating they were close. Caedon hopped off Libra to walk them the rest of the way. He held the reins with his right hand, placing his left on Luna's ankle. The touch was slight, completely subconscious, yet it sent a wave of tranquility up her leg and to her heart. They approached the vacant cabin and Caedon helped her off Libra.

She went inside while he tied the stallion to a nearby tree. Quickly tending to the hearth, Luna searched for a match to light the wood. She turned to the table when she heard the door open and saw Caedon's silhouette in the doorway. His regal posture and magnetic frame caused her to lose her breath.

"I have a match," he said, ignorant of her awe as he made his way to the hearth. Soon, the room was aglow and they were seated at the table.

"As I told you, the people in the village where my parents met were always slightly suspicious of my mother, with her dark, gypsy features and unconventional customs. However, true conjecture did not begin until about three months before her death, when she came home distraught about something. I remember her and my father quarreled, but it was because whatever my mother told him greatly angered him and she did not want him to avenge her. I did not understand it then, but now, now that I have met him, I know."

"Who?" Caedon whispered, his eyes intently focused on her words.

"Father Geirnuk."

They both sat still while Caedon studied her face. His gaze swept over her forehead, cheekbones, jawline and nose before landing on her eyes, now darkened to a charcoal gray. She answered his unspoken question.

"Yes. I fear the worst happened between them. She trusted him like family. Her allure and magnetism seemed to make villagers suspicious, but I do not believe she ever divulged her thoughts on religion and life, which would have assuredly been considered blasphemous. I am not sure what exactly transpired, but looking back on it, recalling her condition when she arrived home – and considering the way Father Geirnuk looks at me now – I can only assume the worst."

"Do you suspect that is why he condemned her? Because she resisted his advances?" Caedon asked, already guessing as much. Luna nodded gravely before bursting into tears. She had not openly and fully sobbed in front of someone since her father's passing. The display felt aberrant. Caedon took her hand and brought her knuckles to his soft lips, warm from his breath. She sniffled, using the handkerchief he had offered to blot her eyes.

"How was she ... ?"

"Burned, at the stake," Luna snapped bitterly, her resentment and anger still raw.

After several minutes, Caedon slightly pushed back in his chair, once again studying Luna's features before reaching into the inner lining of his coat to pull out a small book, its pages yellowed and brittle with age.

"This is my mother's journal. I found it in that trunk I told you about that my father takes with him everywhere. She mentions Cybele."

Luna's heart jumped, their mothers' acquaintanceship further proven.

"She speaks of their connection. They met only a few times, but shared something ... something not of this realm," he said carefully. "She expressed how fearful your mother was − not of her own doomed fate, but of what was to befall you. Just as she told you, she was uncertain of what specifically was to transpire. However, both she and my mother felt the same daunting presence, like a shadow lurking in the corners of every room, just a breath away from your neck."

His eyes grew stormy as his words darkened.

"You see, my mother believed, just as you and I have discovered, that our souls are intertwined. But we are tied to a past neither of us is consciously privy to, nor do we have control over it."

"You mean, your mother believes we have been through something like this before? In another lifetime?"

"Not just my mother, Luna. Yours as well."

Luna could not deny it. Her mother had expressed similar notions, though Duchess Lucinda's contained more detail.

"And, I presume they both believe the outcome was ill-fated."

Caedon's mouth twitched, yet he remained a statue of control. Luna nodded, more to herself than him.

"Both of our mothers believed themselves to be related in a past life, possibly sisters. At least, that is what my mother hypothesized. Both of our mothers talked of karma, the idea that every action has a consequence, good or bad, it has a ripple effect on the future and can create someone's destiny, in this lifetime or the next. And apparently, they believed you and I to be twin flames, two halves of one soul, living out the karma − both positive and negative − of past lives. And because we are each one half of the same soul, we are and will always be drawn to each other. We mirror each other. What happens to one, impacts the other."

Luna swallowed in disbelief; speechless as she processed everything Caedon was telling her. While her mind could not fully fathom the notions he spoke of, something in her heart stirred with every word he uttered as though it was coming alive, as though it was whispering "yes."

"Our mothers," Caedon continued, "they believed we were all linked. It is a lineage of sorts, almost like a bloodline, but on a soul level. And that you and I have been tasked – or cursed as I see it – to live out the sins of not only our past lives, but those of the entire lineage, as though we are a chosen martyr, but split in two. Our lives – our purpose – is much greater than just us. My mother said she had a vision once and it showed me, but I did not look like myself. She said my eyes were mine, but my body was another's. She said I had died saving you, and she had the feeling this was not the first time.

"I know this sounds like lunacy. Maybe they both truly were unwell, but this is what my mother and your mother believed. It is all right here on these pages. And I have to tell you Luna, as I read them, my logical mind bucked at every word, but something deep inside me – that same something that stirred awake the moment I laid eyes on you – it tells me there is truth here. It tells me why I have wanted to be by your side from the moment I met you, almost as though my name and title – this entire life – is some illusion, some skin I am wearing, and why when I look at you, I feel as though I am home. It is the same force inside of me that desires to save you every single time I've known you were in danger. Do you not feel it?"

Finally, Caedon tore his eyes away from the pages of his mother's journal and looked up at Luna, his gaze fierce as he searched her eyes for an answer.

Luna turned her eyes to look into the fire. Tears, lit by the flames, seared down her cheeks.

After what seemed an eternity, she turned to look back at Caedon.

"So, how can we sever the bond?"

Caedon's brow creased, a flash of hurt in his eyes.

"I am not sure we can," he said, his voice grave.

Luna nodded again, accepting his answer. He was finally being honest, instead of painfully optimistic. They could try to convince people otherwise, hoping the duke and the king, if it came down to it, would rather concentrate on ironing out treaty policies than concerning themselves with seemingly trivial sacrilegious accusations. However, with Darius and the priest as the driving force, utilizing the threat of panic amongst the people, it might be near impossible.

Feeling that familiar nebulous pit in her stomach, Luna leaned toward Caedon, urging him to continue.

"My mother also wrote of her own impending demise. After Cybele was killed, even though my mother kept their association a secret from everyone, she mourned her. She mourned for you, even though she had never met you – at least, not in this lifetime," he said, watching Luna's eyes brim with fresh tears. "And she mourned for me because she knew what would eventually come, at least of our paths crossing. While she wrote how I would be altered, that it would be excruciatingly beautiful, she also spoke of the painful aftermath. I fear we are beginning to feel it now."

Luna's tears spilled over as she buried her face in her hands, slowly shaking her head.

"But these are not the passages that struck my heart with a blade so sharp, I have bled for days," Caedon said, his voice solemn.

Luna looked up from her hands, catching a shimmer of menace in his narrowed pupils. It caused a shudder throughout her body.

"I had had my suspicions about my mother's *illness*, but I was so overcome with anguish and misery after her passing, I curled up within myself, never allowing anyone or anything else in again … that is, until you. I let go of my suspicions until I grew older and the divide in my family became more and more apparent. But it was not until now, until reading her words …"

He trailed off, losing his bearings as he hunched forward and cried. His shoulders shook with each wave of sorrow, leaving Luna completely in shock. She had caught glimpses behind his reserve but nothing to this magnitude. Overcome by an incredible urge to heal him, Luna stood up, hovered overtop of him and wrapped her entire upper body around his shoulders and back.

The moment her body melted into his, his sorrows began to ebb, until he was left drained, sniffling and wiping his eyes with that same handkerchief he had lent to her. He straightened up inside her arms until his eyes found hers. Intensity never before seen burned in them. Luna gasped slightly but did not waver.

She was not afraid of him either.

"My mother's words validated what I had always known," he said.

"And what was that?" Luna asked in a hoarse whisper.

"She was murdered ... by my brother."

Chapter 22

Like languid molasses crawling down the bark of a tree, the next moments dragged by in silence. The lump in Luna's throat grew with each passing second. Caedon had his eyes shut tight, as if wishing to close out everything around him. Luna waited, knowing he would continue when he was ready.

After what seemed like an eternity, he opened his damp eyelashes and stared into the fire, its flames licking the top of the hearth.

"It was poison," he said, his voice gravelly with emotion. "She just became sicker and sicker. The doctor could not pinpoint the cause and my father acted oblivious. In fact, part of me had believed he thought it was her punishment for such blasphemous thoughts, and perhaps had even wished it."

Caedon's hands balled into fists, causing Luna to pull back slightly, though her arms remained around him.

"Do you think your father ..." she began, trailing off at the wickedness of the thought.

Caedon shrugged.

"I do not think he knew about the poison, though I think all those years of his ramblings about our mother being possessed by an evil spirit, being cursed, may have supplied my brother with the cryptic notion that this was what he wanted, that our father might be proud of him for doing what he did."

Luna nodded, understanding Caedon's logic. Her father had always told her people who lived in fear, who let it consume them, are capable of anything. Those ghostly words brushed across her mind, sending a shiver down her spine.

"Did Lucinda not say something to your father, to you or to the doctor?" Luna asked.

"She tried. She tried to tell our father that she thought someone might be adding something to her food that was making her sick, though I do not think she ever told him she suspected Darius.

Perhaps she was afraid of the retaliation. My father is quite terrifying when he loses his temper," Caedon recalled, shivering at the thought. "By the time she wrote down her qualms in the journal, the poison had done its worst and she knew she had only days left."

"When did you suspect any of this?" Luna asked.

"Well, at the time, though the doctors called it a mysterious illness, my heart told me differently. I could not fathom anything more, so I buried it in the back of my mind for many years, knowing she was gone and there was nothing I could do to change that. However, as time passed and Darius became more and more isolated, disturbed and jealous, my suspicions resurfaced. I searched for something, anything tangible to use against him to support my theory, but had nothing.

"It was not until I met you, until I looked into your eyes and caught a glimpse of my mother in them, that I remembered the journal tucked away with a few of her remaining belongings. They are the only pieces of her we have left, but my broken heart has never had the strength to look at them all these years. It was as though she spoke to me through you, reminding me of memories I had long since locked away."

Luna shook her head slowly, awestruck by the tale. Now both of their darkest secrets were unveiled, and still, neither felt the relief that should have followed.

Suddenly, another piece of the puzzle slipped into place as Caedon watched Luna's eyes widen, illuminated by the crackling firelight.

"That is what Darius meant, was it not? When he said, 'I knew she would return.' He meant Lucinda. He saw her in my eyes, too."

Caedon grimly nodded.

"I suspect you are a kind of medium. Your eyes are like none I have ever seen," he said, shaking his head for emphasis. "They lighten, to almost a silvery gray when you are at peace or elated in some way. But when you grow angry ... "

Caedon swallowed hard but held her gaze.

"They darken, they become almost as black as onyx. And, perhaps it was a trickery of the light, but I swear, I have seen flames appear in them," he said.

Out of habit, Luna cast her eyes to the floor, afraid of what they were currently showing, but Caedon lifted her face up to his.

"It is nothing to be ashamed of. They are the most magical part of you. They tell a thousand tales without you uttering a single word. They allowed me to see my mother again. How on earth could you think that is something to be ashamed of?"

Luna bit her lower lip, afraid to speak, but felt a single tear escape her left eye as Caedon's thumb gently brushed it away.

"My father would tell me he always spoke to my mother when he looked into my eyes," Luna said, her voice cracking with emotion. "I did not realize the truth behind that until now. It is as though my eyes are a gateway to another realm."

In one fierce, swift motion, Caedon pulled Luna onto his lap, bringing her lips crushing against his. The piercing wave of heat hit them at once, causing Luna to let out a soft moan, while Caedon groaned, burying his hands in her hair. After a few moments of passion, Luna gently pulled back, breaking the kiss. Caedon's eyes remained closed, as though under a spell.

"We must go back, you know," she whispered, finally breaking the enchantment. His eyes flew open and steadily met hers before he nodded in agreement. They slowly stood up, though never broke from their embrace, and stared into the hearth. The flames had dissipated, leaving only glowing embers in their wake.

*****

It was well past nightfall when Luna finally got back to the servants' wing. Almost everyone had retired for the evening.

Almost everyone.

"What on earth is going on Luna?" Katrin demanded in a gruff whisper, her brow furrowed with worry and anger.

"Trust me. The less you know, the better," Luna said, attempting to pass her as she stood in the doorway to the sleeping quarters.

"You must tell me something. Do you know His Grace Darius and the magistrate from your village were here today? They wanted access to your belongings!"

Luna's mind reeled from Katrin's words. Why would they want to see her belongings? What on earth would they be looking for?

"Did you allow them?" she asked, trying to keep a low, steady voice.

"Well, of course, Luna. I had no choice. They said they would alert the duke and then the king if they had to."

Luna nodded, knowing it was not Katrin's fault and that displacing her anger would not help matters.

"And what came of it?"

"Not much that I could tell, though they left with one of your blouses in hand."

Luna's stomach dropped, her mind instantly flashing back to Darius' hand holding that torn piece of cloth, taunting her with it. But what would they do? Accuse her of killing the gypsy man? How could they possibly link the two from a piece of cloth?

Her mind raced with possibilities as Katrin's eyes narrowed on her. Realizing her prolonged silence, Luna snapped out of her state, managing to muster a few words.

"I have no idea what they suspect Katrin, but I can tell you that Darius has it in for me because I saved Arianna from his vile grasp," Luna spat, her patience wearing thin.

"Luna! How can you speak so ill of the duke's son?" Katrin gasped.

"Because it is the truth. Ask Arianna yourself if you do not believe me," Luna said tersely. "Now, can I please retire to my bed? It has been a very long, trying day and I am afraid of what tomorrow will bring."

As if sensing she was holding on to her sanity by a thread, Katrin backed off, content for now. She stepped aside, letting Luna pass, though her probing eyes didn't leave Luna's back until the door closed behind her.

Morning came quickly and Luna found she had slept the whole night through, possibly from sheer exhaustion. She briskly washed up, dressed and decided to go to the servants stables to feed the horses before she helped Katrin with the day's chores.

Maybe it was the idea that if she continued about the day as normally as possible, everything else would fade away, or maybe she just needed to do something mundane to keep her mind steady. Either way, Luna found herself in the stables before sunrise, methodically pouring feed into each stall.

She was so entranced by her own motions, she did not even hear the stable door open and close, or the slowly approaching footfalls. It was not until a familiar tingle shot through her veins that Luna was finally pulled from the lull of her work.

"My dearest Luna, you are looking very well this morning," Darius said, his words slithering up her skin.

"I cannot say the same for you," she replied with disgust, noting his unkempt appearance, the dark circles under his eyes, his unshaven face and disheveled hair.

"I was not afforded sleep last night, like you. I was awake, listening to foul accusations being spewed at me by my own traitor brother!" He spat. "And what is worse? He woke my father to repeat those atrocious lies!"

Luna stood her ground, though her legs were shaking beneath her skirt. Darius seemed oblivious to her reactions for the moment, more caught up in his own emotional outburst.

"What's more, he planned to show him our mother's journal," he said with a nervous chuckle. "What a joke. My father, who had so much contempt and resentment toward my mother, had never bothered to take any of her mad ravings seriously, let alone read anything she wrote. Or if he had, he recognized them for what they were – lunacy. He merely keeps her belongings with him to remind him of what happens when our minds break under the influence of the Devil. Nevertheless, these memories are best left buried, dearest Luna. So I got to her journal when my brother was in the bath and I have since destroyed it."

Luna's stomach sank as all hope diminished before her eyes, while Darius' smile widened.

"But I noticed a few pages were missing," he continued in a child-like tone. "I thought about who might be devious enough to take them. I thought about the things I saw in your eyes, Luna, and realized it was you."

Darius took a step closer, swiftly closing the space between them, and grabbed Luna's wrist.

"Where are they?" he growled softly, now letting his eyes revel in her reactions. But she was determined to give him no satisfaction. She found a sliver of peace, deep within her, as she pictured her father's pale blue eyes bathing her in their love.

Darius' forehead creased in confusion at her serene expression and he tightened his grip on her wrist, cutting into her circulation. She remained steady, though that peace was waning.

"I do not know what you are talking about," she said, hoping he could see in her eyes she was telling the truth. But she knew he had finally gone mad. She saw it in his vacant yet crazed eyes. Whatever darkness shackled him all these years had finally consumed him.

"You are just like my whore of a mother, always enchanting men, making them stray from God's path, cursing them. But I will not let you bewitch me, you heathen. Just as I did not let my mother sink her sinful claws into me," he rambled, his grip causing Luna to lose feeling in her hand. She winced slightly, making him groan with pleasure.

"Let me go," she said softly, though her eyes were already dimming as she felt adrenaline begin to course through her body. Her abdominal muscles tensed beneath her blouse as her legs prepared for attack.

"Father Geirnuk was once enchanted. It was by your mother," he said, momentarily catching Luna off guard. "Her mere presence caused unholy thoughts to seep into his mind. He knew when he saw you that you carried her curse and that you must suffer her fate. The same fate as my mother."

"You are ludicrous, Darius. I am not my mother. I am my own being. I believe in and love God just as you do. I have not hurt anyone!" Luna screamed.

"You liar! I found your blouse that matched the piece of cloth found on the gypsy. You killed him! I know you did."

"I did not. He attacked me. I fought and his heart gave out from the strain. How could I have caused that?" Luna asked, her voice cracking with emotion.

"It is inside you. It is the same thing that changes your eyes, that sets your skin aflame," Darius seethed. "It is the same thing that has burned those you have touched in anger. You see, Luna, after my discussions with your village's magistrate, he reexamined that gypsy's body. He opened him right up. He said while the man's external body appeared normal, save for the burn on his wrist, his insides looked as though they had been boiled. Boiled! How on earth could such a thing be true? It is witchery. It is the work of the Devil! And you nearly killed me with it, too!"

Luna violently shook her head as tears streamed down her face. Darius grabbed her face by the chin, bringing his eyes inches from her, his acrid breath upon her lips.

"But now, I am going to kill you."

Chapter 23

Slowly wrapping his long fingers around Luna's throat, Darius pushed her hard up against the stall. With lungs screaming for air, Luna gasped, writhing her body against his, but he did not budge. Using the door behind her for support, Luna lifted her legs up and kicked out as hard as she could.

Darius momentarily loosened his grip on her neck, giving her a chance to fill her lungs as he keeled over in pain. She tried to flee his grasp, but he tackled her, sending them both to the hard dirt-covered floor as dust billowed out around them. Taking a wrist with each hand, Darius pinned her to the floor, sitting on her lower half.

Suddenly time stood still, the only sound was Luna's coarse, quickened breaths and the rapid rise and fall of her chest. Darius stared at her, his eyes black with menace and excitement as they scoured the length of her.

"You caught my brother's eye. No one has ever caught his eye, not even someone as fair as Duchess Rosalind," Darius whispered through rapid breaths. "We thought, at one point, perhaps he was not interested in the female sex at all. He snubbed his nose at everyone, including our own father, who still treated him like gold and would give him anything he asked for. How ironic he was bewitched by a lowly, whore of a servant."

Darius shook his head, his voice rising with hysteria.

"He lived each day going through the motions, bored with life, bored with everyone and everything around him. And yet my father adored him. Not once did he offer his title to me. Not once, even after my brother practically spit it back in his face."

Luna's breathing steadily slowed as she half-listened and half-searched for a way out of her compromised position.

"But now my father will see. He knows about you and he has already rebuked Caedon, calling him weak, tainted, subservient to your guiles," Darius said, a wicked grin spreading across his face, tightening around ominous eyes. "But not me. Your scent, your very essence may have tried to seduce me, but I have more restraint than my brother. The moment I discovered what you were, I freed myself. I knew, then, I needed to rid the world of you."

As though realizing his mouth had run away with him, Darius' eyes narrowed in on a very calm Luna. His head cocked to the side with curiosity, but she remained eerily still. Sensing something brooding inside her, Darius shifted his weight backward, crushing her pelvis beneath him. She winced slightly, but stayed quiet, cringing inwardly as she felt his arousal.

"But you still try, do you not?" he asked, increasing pressure on her wrists. Luna began shaking her head, desperation getting the better of her.

"Yes, yes you do," he whispered, bringing his mouth to her neck, biting it roughly. She squeezed her eyes shut and bit her lip to keep from screaming.

"Well, I am going to make sure you never use your witchery on another soul," he said before crushing her neck with both hands. Stars burst before her eyes as Luna clawed at his fingers. She felt her skin burn beneath them, causing Darius to gasp incredulously before applying pressure once more.

"Those are the eyes," he growled, watching Luna's irises darken to stormy pools of gray, as flames began to dance in them. They started to roll back as she struggled to maintain consciousness. Darius' eyes grew wide with wild fascination as he watched her and felt a burning pain sear through his hands.

Suddenly, he caught his breath and propelled forward while clutching at his heart and stomach. Luna rolled him to her side while scurrying to get up. Just as she gained balance, she felt a hand grasp her ankle, causing her to trip forward, gashing her forehead on a stray pebble. The horses in the barn grew restless, chattering nervously as Darius crawled toward her.

Just as she opened her mouth to scream out, he clasped his palm over her lips, shoving her bleeding head to the ground.

"I will not be killed that easily," he snarled, unsheathing a knife he hid beneath his vestments. He brought it to her throat, drawing blood as he gently sliced the skin just under her chin. Fortunately, it was only a flesh wound. Luna let out a muffled cry beneath his hand, as her hands clenched into fists at her side.

"Darius!" Caedon's voice thundered against the stall doors behind them. "If you do not release her, you will have a dagger lodged inside your skull."

Darius' eyes grew wide at the threat, briefly awestruck by Caedon's temper. He neither released her, nor moved the knife from her throat, but he raised his head slightly, staring at the ground a few inches from Caedon's boots.

"She is evil, brother. She has charmed you into believing you have feelings for her, into protecting her, but she's malevolent. She just tried to kill me, like she killed that vagrant gypsy!"

"Let her go," Caedon said, leveling his tone as he pivoted to the side, catching a glimpse of Luna's terrified eyes. His jaw flexed with pained anger as he watched Darius' grip tighten on the dagger.

"Do you not see Caedon?! The priest sees. The magistrate sees. Even father sees! How can you not?"

"She is not the cold-blooded killer, Darius. You are," Caedon growled.

At his words, Darius flinched, finally turning to look at his brother, yet careful to keep the knife pressed against Luna's neck.

Caedon paused a moment and then took a gamble, lunging at his brother and knocking Darius to the side before he was able to slit Luna's throat. Sitting up, quickly edging her way backward from the wrestling brothers, Luna brought her hands to her neck, making sure the damage was not too severe.

She watched in horror as Caedon and Darius struggled with the knife.

"Run," Caedon yelled at her, straddling Darius while wrestling the knife away from him.

"I cannot leave you," Luna cried, tears instantly pouring down her face. Her words only seemed to make Darius angrier as he flipped Caedon over his head while stripping him of his dagger.

"She had to die. She would have killed us all," Darius rasped, trying to catch his breath as he and Caedon both cautiously rose to their feet. Caedon's eyes flitted over to Luna, who was also now standing. They silently pleaded for her to leave, but she shook her head, feeling fresh tears stream down her cheeks.

"But I knew she would come back to haunt me," Darius said. "And I must kill her once and for all."

"You have truly lost your mind brother," Caedon said, the pity he felt for Darius finally showing in his eyes.

But Darius saw nothing, his crazed pupils now fixed on Luna, who felt a force inside of her take over.

"Do not touch her!" Caedon screamed as Darius lunged for her, the dagger aimed at her chest. Luna's hand shot out a mere second before the blade hit, flipping it up and backward in a flash.

She felt Darius crash into her, his face inches from hers as his eyes opened wide in horror. Her hands felt warm liquid as she realized his forward momentum had thrust the blade straight into his sternum.

Luna's right hand, still on his chest, was burning. She watched Darius' skin turn dark red, as boils appeared on his face and neck.

Slowly, he slid down the length of her, leaving a trail of blood down her skirt.

Luna screamed.

Chapter 24

It was not until Caedon carried Luna outside and into the other stables that she realized she had fainted. Her cheeks burned with the salt from her tears.

Seeing she had come to, Caedon set her on her feet while he secured a saddle on Libra along with a canteen of water and loaf of bread.

"What are you doing?" she said through shaky lips.

Caedon said nothing as he tightened the girth around Libra's expansive ribcage.

"Caedon," she said, her voice gaining strength as she took deep breaths to settle her nerves.

"We have to get out of here," he said, his voice clipped with tension.

"And go where? They'll find us. They'll find us no matter where we go. Your father will involve the king once he finds Darius," Luna said, setting a hand on his shoulder. He shrugged it off and continued to pull the leather strap around the horse tighter.

"I have to at least get you out of here," he said.

"And what? Leave you to handle the aftermath? They'll charge you with murder. Or they'll punish you for aiding me," Luna said, her voice defeated.

Caedon finally turned toward her and looked into her eyes.

"My father is King Bertrem's right-hand man. He will not do anything to me."

"Are you so naive to think they will not accuse me of being a witch and you of being cursed or of being an accessory? Do you not see that the panic it will cause will be enough for the king to send you to jail – or worse – in order to quiet villagers' cries? Especially during peace agreements. He would never allow a disturbance of this nature, Caedon. The fears of sorcery may have dissipated over the years in certain parts of these lands, but they still bubble under the surface. I saw what just the whisper of a threat did to my mother. Your father may be close to the king, but King Bertrem beheaded his own brother based on rumors of a planned betrayal. Rumors! He did not even have proof – "

Caedon shushed her with a gentle touch of his hand to her lips, causing Luna to realize she had been bordering on hysteria.

"We will figure something out. But for now, we need to at least get away from here and find shelter."

Luna did not have to ask to know what Caedon had in mind. As far as the king and anyone else were concerned, the cabin was the last place they would think to look – a long forgotten haven. They quickly reached the edge of the forest, taking one last look at the king's castle. At any moment now, someone would find Darius' bloody remains, the dagger missing. Luna shuddered, and Caedon tightened his grip around her waist, urging Libra into the gnarled woods.

As they drew closer to the cabin, the sun's rays grew stronger, beating down on them through the trees. Libra's hide was dewy with sweat as they approached the pond Luna had once fallen asleep near. How peaceful and safe her life had been then. How perilous it seemed now.

Oh Mama, Papa, why did you not tell me? Why did you not prepare me?

Libra's abrupt halt pulled Luna from her thoughts as she realized they were at the cabin. Caedon reached up to help her down, reminding her of the first time he had done so and how her heart had raced. Caedon seemed to be thinking the same, a ghost of a smile on his lips.

As they entered the cabin, Luna felt a chill. She pulled her mother's heavy wrap tighter around her shoulders as Caedon went over to the hearth to start a fire. It felt as though they had a pattern now. As if this place was theirs.

After the fire built to a roaring blaze, Caedon cut up some bread at the table, offering Luna a slice along with the canteen of water. She shook her head, her knotted, anxious stomach curling from the sight of food. But she did take a swill of water, reveling in its iciness as it flooded her stomach.

A few moments passed before Caedon extracted the dagger from under his tunic, Darius' dried blood catching in the firelight. Luna almost lost the water she had just ingested when Caedon covered the blade with a cloth, bound it with straw and lifted a loose floorboard under the table. He poured dirt over it, placed the board back and used a heavy stone to beat the nails more firmly into place.

Luna's hands stopped trembling the moment the last nail was secured, but as her eyes trailed over her fingers, wrists and clothing, the quivering began again at the sight of Darius' dark, crimson blood.

Caedon filled a small basin with water from the pond and used a cloth to wipe Luna's skin clean. His eyes searched hers, but they were vacant. He carried her to the bed where she then laid, staring up at the ceiling.

"I killed him. Oh my God," she whispered. "I killed your brother."

"No Luna, you defended yourself. He would have killed you," Caedon abruptly corrected.

"But he is your brother," Luna said, her voice barely audible. Caedon briskly shook his head.

"He has not been my brother in a very, very long time, Luna," he said, sadly.

"But I did not even realize what I had done. It was as though something else overtook me, moved my hand to react in such an unnatural way."

Caedon sat next to her on the bed, moving a tendril of hair from her eyes as he softly shook his head in disagreement.

"That was not the way of it. Your instincts took over, just as they do for anyone trying to survive. If you did not react, he would have killed you."

"Maybe that would have been the better result," Luna whispered.

Caedon's hand briskly but gently clamped over her mouth.

"Do not dare talk like that. You are a gift, Luna. You are precious, not evil. Those who love you, who have raised you, are they not as loyal as anyone could be?"

Luna thought of sweet, loving Dirdra and steadfast, protective Regan and her heart swelled with pain. Tears flowed from her eyes, streaming down to meet the side of Caedon's hand, still resting over her lips. What she would give to see Dirdra again, to smell her sweet bread in the oven, her chicken stew over the hearth ... and to hug Regan, to walk the grounds with her again.

Shaking her head slightly, Luna focused back on Caedon's tender eyes.

"They see the gift you are. I see the gift you are. You have opened me up to things in this life I had thought a figment of my imagination. Some of them, I never even knew existed at all. Just because people fear something different, something profound, and feeble-minded men do not know how to process it, to be near it without letting it overwhelm them, does not mean you are a malevolent curse. You are the most beautifully fierce creature I have ever encountered."

Caedon removed his hand from her jaw, offering his handkerchief for her to wipe her eyes. He watched as she looked down at her tarnished blouse, cringing at the sight of blood that was blackening as it dried.

Pulling her to sit up, Caedon gently tugged the handkerchief from her grip and brought his hands to her sides. Gathering handfuls of cloth on both sides, Caedon slowly, steadily pulled up. Luna's breath caught as she realized what he was doing, but she let him continue, desperate to be free of the soiled blouse.

With nothing left but her sheer undergarment, Luna wrapped her arms around herself as Caedon laid her back down and began to work on her skirt. Unsure if it was nerves, a deep yearning, or both, Luna's legs began to shiver beneath the cloth. Caedon felt the trembling and stopped, looking up at her.

"It is alright," she said, causing him to resume sliding the skirt down the length of her body, leaving only her thin underskirt in its wake.

Caedon went to the basin, soaking a cloth rag with more water and brought it over to her, bringing it down to her collarbones. The languid, circular motion was both soothing and sensual as Caedon ran the coarse fabric over her skin, the water dripping down her sides. This could be the last time she feels his touch, Luna realized, closing her eyes so she could burn it to her memory. Perhaps they were both losing their minds after the shock of what just happened. Perhaps they were completely mad with emotion, tension and fear. But something snapped inside Luna. She felt desperate to hold onto this moment forever. Feeling her chest tighten beneath the cloth, Luna's hand shot up, stopping Caedon.

Her eyes opened, locking onto his sparkling sapphire irises. They intently devoured her as she threw the damp cloth aside and pulled him on top of her. His lips crashed into hers, causing fire to trickle down her spine and into her toes.

Her fingers nimbly worked at his tunic, pulling it loose from his waist and over his head. The motion revealed a bare back and chest, their curves catching in the dancing firelight. Luna's breath caught as she gazed at him, his eyes fixed on her face, neckline and collarbones.

Caedon's unspoken question bore into her eyes, as Luna's heart quickened its pulse, heating her body. She swallowed and nodded, afraid her voice would only come out an inaudible whisper. It was not that she was afraid. Every ounce of her felt at home in Caedon's arms. But she was nervous, unsure of what her body would do.

Caedon misread her anxiety, beginning to cautiously back away, but Luna stopped him with a firm grip.

"I am just worried about ... about my body," she said in a raspy whisper. Caedon's concerned eyes softened instantly.

"I am not sure how I know this, but I have a feeling I can handle anything you have," he said, a slight smirk on his lips. Luna smiled at his self-assuredness and pulled him toward her.

She finished undressing him, her face flushing at the sight of his completely naked form as she reflexively looked down at the bed sheets. Caedon gently placed his hand beneath her chin, raising her eyes to meet his.

"Are you sure?" he whispered, his voice raw with desire.

"Yes," she said.

Caedon pulled off the rest of her undergarments, holding his breath as his eyes cascaded down the length of her.

"You are the most beautiful creature I have ever seen," he breathed.

Luna resisted the urge to curl into a ball under his overwhelming gaze, but remained still, half turned toward him with her one hip slightly higher than the other. He lifted the sheet and they slid under as he pulled her body into his arms, pressing up against her sensuous skin.

A slow sigh escaped them almost simultaneously as Caedon inhaled her scent, burying his face in her hair.

"You smell of vanilla ... and honey," he said, nuzzling her neck, kissing just below her ear to cause a stream of gooseflesh down her side.

She moaned slightly as Caedon's mouth kissed down her jawline before engulfing her lips. They let the kiss linger, enjoying the feel of each other's tongues exploring the deepest regions of their mouths. Then Caedon kissed Luna's collarbones, lightly grazing her breasts, before moving down her torso. She unconsciously arched her back, causing a groan to escape his throat.

"Your scent is tantalizing," he breathed into her skin, sliding both of his hands up her thighs, feeling her skin burning beneath them. Sweat began to bead on both of their brows, but Caedon savored the heat, enjoying its searing sensation.

As Luna's thighs quivered beneath his touch, Caedon began to tremble as well.

"What is the matter?" she asked, shyly gazing beneath her lashes at his eyes.

"Nothing. Nothing at all," he said through raspy breaths before plunging back into her lips with a fierceness neither anticipated. Luna dug her fingernails into his back and slowly dragged them down his sides as she felt his entire body rigid beneath them, throbbing with energy.

Without another word, Luna parted her legs, pulling Caedon's body between them. He searched her eyes, but stopped before pushing farther.

Time seemed to halt, muting the crackling fire and filling the room with a piercing silence.

"I love you."

Tears brimmed Caedon's eyes as the words burst out of him in a wave of emotion.

Luna's translucent eyes filled as well, her body pulsing with warmth. The image of her eyes in that moment was haunting.

"I love you," she whispered with raw emotion.

He thrust his hips forward, feeling the give as she took all of him inside her. Her face tightened at first, before her entire body practically burst into flames. Her eyes snapped open to find Caedon's eyes wide, his mouth slightly parted in awe. As they slowly moved into each other, Caedon felt as though his skin were aflame, his nerve endings seared by the painful pleasure.

He rolled to his side, pulling her on top of him, reveling in the shadows dancing across her angelic, porcelain skin as they accentuated her dark, swollen lips and burnished, chestnut hair. His hands on her hips, Caedon etched every curve, every scent, every feeling into his mind's eye.

Feeling pressure building in them both, Caedon held back, locking his gaze on hers as he felt her body go rigid before rupturing into waves of pleasure. She let out a raspy moan, which only grew more forceful with every convulsion.

Just as the final wave hit, Caedon released, feeling his taut body slacken with each movement. Luna fell onto his damp chest, letting her hair tumble down his sides. She felt the rise and fall of his body as he regained his breath, while she quivered with the aftereffects of their passion.

Rolling onto her side, Luna laid her head against the inside of his upper arm and gazed up at him.

"Thank you," she whispered.

Caedon looked at her astonished as he watched her lips spread into a serene smile while her eyes filled with fresh tears.

"It was perfect," she said, her voice thick with emotion.

Caedon gently wiped her eyes with his thumb, kissed her forehead and parted his lips against it.

"Because it was us."

Chapter 25

Feeling a deep peace, both Luna and Caedon fell into a tranquil sleep. It was nightfall when they awoke and the silvery light from the full moon poured through the window, blanketing them in its effervescence.

Caedon felt Luna stir and immediately pulled her into his arms. He glanced at the hearth and realized the fire was almost out. Gently, he unraveled himself from her and the bed sheets to put another log on the dimming embers. He felt time's merciless grasp upon his neck, but chose to bask in the moment instead, with a sense of foreboding about something to come.

"How much time do we have?" Luna's raspy voice mumbled as she slowly came to. Caedon shook his head, hoping if he did not speak, nothing would change.

Deciding she also did not want to think of what was to come, Luna put her arm out, beckoning Caedon back to the warm bed. He complied and was again entangled in her arms. She pressed her cheek against his shoulder as she turned her silvery eyes to meet his.

They reminded her then of her father's eyes and she stifled a sudden wave of tears. How she longed for him, how he would have found a way to protect her. But he would have wanted to run, just as they had before. And just as the past had caught up to them now, it would again. However, this time, she had done much worse. She had blood on her hands.

Caedon sensed the forlorn shift in Luna's emotions and pulled her more tightly against him. The moonbeams made her eyes almost translucent now as he studied her jawline and furrowed brow.

"You know, I have been thinking," Luna said. "Before you came, Darius told me the magistrate re-examined that gypsy man's body and that his insides looked like they had been burned from the inside. While I do not understand how, I know, in my heart, I did that. Something inside of me did that, and whatever it is, it is directly tied to my emotions. If we entertain our mothers' thoughts a moment – if, as they said, we are two halves of one soul, and if we have been brought back, over and over again, for the purpose of clearing all of our karmas – how is it I can do the things I do with my body and mind and you cannot?"

Caedon mulled over her words, processing the new information about the old man's cause of death, as well as Luna's ensuing question.

"Firstly," he began, "yes, it would seem your fire is tied to your emotions. However, as far as we know, it seems to only take over when you are in need of protection. As for your question, perhaps you are looking at it in the wrong way. Perhaps it's more like polarity with one end active and the other passive. You see, when I've touched you, when you've burned up, for instance, just after Darius died, I felt it, but it never hurt me. In fact, I felt like the moment I touched you, your fire dissipated. Let me ask you something. Did your mother have this ability?"

"I am not sure. I know my mother had an effect on people, and not just men. It was almost as though she was hypnotic, like she could get people to do what she asked them with just the look in her eyes. She also had a temper at times, which only added fuel to her influence. But not my father, he would often be a voice of reason. He was always a calming force in our home. His eyes were blue, like yours. In fact, now that we are talking about it, every time I felt my body heat up, I would instinctively think of my father's eyes and they would immediately calm my body, similarly to how I feel when I'm around you."

Caedon smiled, as they both continued to put pieces of this mystifying puzzle together.

"So perhaps your father was in your mother's life to be a balancing, neutralizing presence to the active elements within her – as I am, to you," he said softly.

"Yes ... perhaps you are right," Luna said, her eyes softening.

They both looked at the fire now, lost in their thoughts. Luna grew frustrated when she thought of her mother and Lucinda.

Why would they have not prepared us for this? Why did they keep us in the dark?

But, the reality was neither Cybele nor Lucinda had known exactly what would transpire and just how catastrophic it would be. And what could they have done? No one would believe them. Furthermore, they would have been condemned for such thoughts had they been spoken aloud.

"I will tell them I killed Darius," Caedon said, his voice reverberated against Luna's skin, startling her from her thoughts.

"You mustn't, Caedon. It was my doing, regardless of the circumstances. You still have a chance, whereas I am doomed no matter what is said."

"You are not. Executions for blasphemy have been subsiding under King Bertrem, despite what was done to your mother or what Father Geirnuk has said," Caedon said softly, encouragement filling every word that vacated his mouth.

Luna nodded, but remained unconvinced. She believed that she was nothing. She was just a servant who may as well not even exist as far as the king was concerned. But Caedon had not thought of the duke and his influence.

"What of your father? He may love you more than he ever loved Darius, but that will not matter when he learns what happened," Luna said, propping up her head for a better look at Caedon's face.

"I will deal with my father. I have seen in your eyes your baffled musings at how I could not feel even an ounce of sadness regarding Darius. Let me be honest in saying I do feel anguish over what has happened, but not because of what you were forced to do. It is what I would have done, had you not. It is because in that moment, when I saw the madness in his eyes, I realized how much I had failed him. Perhaps I could have done something as we were growing up, when our mother was alive and before his mind became sick with jealousy and hatred, to prevent what happened to her – and what is happening to us."

"Just me," Luna said softly, a tear escaping her eye. Caedon's hand flew to her lips, hushing them.

"No. I am in this with you. And if you say something to the contrary again, I will have to resort to finding a way to keep you from talking at all."

His mouth curved into a slight smirk, causing Luna to momentarily forget their woes and smile in return. How much she loved that smile and how rare it was for him to give.

"Do you think maybe it is possible to change our fate? Maybe our mothers were granted the foresight so that we could find a way to alter our path. Maybe we will be able to save ourselves," she said, her eyes desperately searching his, eager to find agreement or even a trace of optimism.

"I do not know. I just know both Cybele and Lucinda had a gift, just as you do. That they were not cursed and neither are you. But perhaps those gifts arrived before their time. Or maybe they completed the roles they were here to fulfill. Maybe we are just lucky to know our souls are connected somehow, to witness a realm of existence that few others can see. Maybe we are before our time."

All these notions made Luna's mind weary. She did not want to pretend she understood what her ability was or what her connection to Caedon meant. It was undeniable they were tied to each other, that they had changed their lives in what seemed an instant.

But to what end? Was our purpose to sacrifice ourselves to fulfill some ancient karma of our pasts? Or was this about something greater than our minds could possibly fathom?

Regardless of lives past, if Luna's instincts told her anything, nothing would save her in the coming hours.

Caedon's hand caressed her cheek, following her sharp jawline until he gently held her chin between his thumb and index fingers.

"You have changed my life, my dear Luna. You made a lifeless, bored, indifferent man know that there is much, much more to feel, taste, touch, see and believe in than most people will ever know," he said, his eyes glazing over with tears. "No matter what happens, I will find a way to save you."

Caedon's eyes penetrated hers, opening up completely so she could see to the deepest regions of his soul. She nodded, deciding to believe him, even if it meant believing in a dream.

Shimmering moonbeams poured through the window, playfully glistening on Luna's eyelashes. Feeling the gentle glow, both Luna and Caedon turned toward the glass, looking up at the large round moon casting shadows around them.

"The moon is as soft as your smile, as smooth as the small of your back, as sultry as your lips, pressed up against my ear in a whisper," Caedon said, his poetic words vibrating against her temple. "She dances on her black tapestry while the stars shine their applause down on her."

"She *is* beautiful," Luna whispered, turning to look into Caedon's eyes.

He pulled her into his arms, bringing his lips tenderly against hers as they both felt a jolt of emotion rip through them. They sunk into the pillow, losing themselves to the sensual, serene pull of their intertwined energies.

But sadly, their exchange was brief. Moments later, Libra stirred and whinnied outside as they heard the steady footfalls that alerted them of someone fast approaching.

As the sound drew nearer, they looked at one another, eyes quickly widening.

It was more the sound of a small militia.

*****

Four loud raps on the door caused them both to jump. Caedon quickly pulled on his clothes. Luna searched for her own before suddenly realizing they had disposed of the bloodstained garments hours earlier. Caedon's eyes widened as the knocks grew into rumbling pounds, followed by a deep voice bellowing his name.

Luna did the only thing she could. She swept the bed sheets around her while pulling her legs in and wrapping her arms around her shins, her petrified eyes glued to the door. Seeing no movement from Caedon, Luna tore her gaze from the thundering knocks to meet his stare.

In that moment, everything went silent as Luna watched Caedon's usual mask of control come unhinged. His brow creased with anguish as he bore into her eyes, the flickering firelight capturing tears that were not there a moment before. The fear was not for himself. It was for her.

He swallowed, his jaw tightly set while his emotions warred with one another before he finally settled on a guise of composure.

Just as suddenly, the moment passed and sound burst into the room, flooding their ears and hearts. The door flew open and two of King Bertrem's armed guards stepped in, followed by Father Geirnuk, Duke Nicolai and the magistrate from Luna's village.

Upon seeing Caedon's unkempt appearance and Luna's indecent state, Father Geirnuk's scathing face flushed red while the duke's eyes narrowed in anger and his hands began to shake.

"How dare you defy me, your brother and your kingdom!" the duke screamed, causing Caedon to wince. "You not only aided this, this murdering, deceiving, wench by bringing her here. You bedded her, further tainting yourself with her wickedness!"

This was the first time Caedon had witnessed his father almost near madness with anger and completely out of control. No one moved, not even the guards, as though everyone was frozen in place by the duke's unexpected outburst.

Finally, his shaking subsided as the priest and magistrate stepped in front of him to address them both.

"You and the girl are to come with us, now. By order of King Bertrem, you are to be held in his prison quarters until further notice," the magistrate said, never once looking at Luna, but instead, reading from the scroll in front of him while briefly glancing up at Caedon.

"She has nothing to do with any of this. I killed Darius!" Caedon growled, moving toward the magistrate, who reflexively stepped back.

Before the duke could utter a sound, Father Geirnuk gripped his arm tightly while the magistrate moved forward again, putting his hand up to silence Caedon.

"Do not speak another word. This is not your trial. We are merely here to collect the two of you until a decision is made," he said, moving slowly toward Caedon as the two guards in the doorway stepped in.

"Fine, take me. But do not touch her," Caedon said through his teeth.

"I'm afraid I have to bring you both in," the magistrate said, almost sounding sincere in his regret. As both guards moved toward Caedon, he realized he was far outnumbered. He chose to remain under control as he let the two men tie his wrists while the stone-faced duke watched.

Shortly after, two more guards walked into the cabin and toward Luna. At first, she began to shrink against the pillows, but as the two men approached and towered over her, she pulled the sheet tighter around her breasts before tucking it into place just under her arm. Watching her every move, the guards hesitated, unsure of touching her. However, as she edged forward on the bed, showing no signs of violence, their tension noticeably softened.

Luna knew this was not the time to fight.

The duke, priest and magistrate backed out of the room as the guards followed, Caedon and Luna in tow.

Caedon glanced back through the open door, seeing the dimming firelight reflect against the bed. A flicker brushed passed a long, ebony scarf cascading off the side of the bed.

Its lacey trim barely grazed the cold, damp floor before a harsh gale descended, slamming the door behind them.

Chapter 26

Luna shifted in the cart, trying to find some semblance of comfort with both hands tied behind her back. A rope tied tightly around her mouth cut into her cheeks, adding to her vexation and making it almost impossible to breathe.

Hearing the crunching hooves of another horse following them, she wondered if Caedon was in a similar state. The sheet she had put on was almost entirely loose around her torso, making it hard for her to move at all for fear of it sliding below her chest.

Time droned on as Luna slipped in and out of consciousness, her frayed nerves forcing her mind to take a break. Her heart ached as she pictured Caedon, though his station may have afforded him more comfortable means of travel than hers.

As obedient as the king's soldiers, the horses abruptly halted at the crack of a whip. Luna heard a key turn and the pop of a lock as an outstretched hand opened her makeshift prison, pouring moonlight in from behind him. The silhouette handed her a familiar peasant skirt and corset top.

She squinted, making out Father Geirnuk's murky green eyes looking at her with disdain. Yet something else was there, deeper, as his gaze momentarily skimmed past her neckline to the sheet, falling dangerously low. She felt, rather than heard, his heart quicken, as he seemed to try and regain himself.

"Here!" he snarled, throwing the clothes at her. She flicked her head to the side, motioning toward her tied hands. He loosened the rope around her mouth, then moved to untie her wrists, bringing his face dangerously close to hers as he leaned in.

"Even now," he whispered, "you remind me so much of her. Even your scent, that hint of vanilla, takes me back to the very day she showed me her true self, when she seduced me right there in the altar."

"You filthy liar," Luna growled as she turned back to face him, her eyes black with rage.

The priest recoiled. The movement was fast, barely foreseeable, but his hand made contact with her cheek before she had time to react.

The impact was met with burning in Luna's eyes. She righted herself long enough to hear rustling from the cart behind them. She knew immediately it was Caedon and he had sensed the altercation. Continuing to glare at the priest, Luna wiggled her wrists free, which sent the sheet tumbling to her waist. Feeling nothing but her hair hiding her breasts, she snatched up the sheet, though the priest never once looked away, knowing it unnerved her.

A moment later, he slammed the cart door shut, sending her back into a world of darkness. She quickly pulled on the clothes as the cart jerked forward once more. She assumed they had just stopped at the castle and were now heading to the prison.

However, not long after they started up again, they stopped.

What now?

Hearing a scuffle, Luna leaned against the door. "Release him!" she heard a woman scream.

The duchess.

"I said let him go, now!" she repeated.

"My Lady, this is a matter for the village to determine and for the king to decide where Caedon is concerned," she heard the duke say, his tone emotionless.

"But I know for a fact he was bewitched by that wretched servant girl, just like Darius," she said, her voice elevated.

"Rosalind!" the duke said, matching her tone.

Silence followed.

The horses picked up once more, but now a third set could be heard following close by.

Luna sighed, feeling as though an anvil rested on her chest.

Yet the steady footfalls were momentary, as Duchess Rosalind's final outburst stopped everyone once again.

"Look! I found her clothes in the cabin. They are drenched in your son's blood!"

This time, the silence seemed to drag on for hours, until Luna felt her cart being unlocked and opened to a face filled with pure hatred.

Duke Nicolai never looked fiercer, his eyes boring into her as he shoved the bloodied cloth in her face, causing her to duck backward and wince.

He reached in, grabbed her by the hair and yanked her to her feet. Luna did not dare make a sound, though her scalp screamed in agony as he took the rope still hanging around her neck and tied it to the back of the cart.

The magistrate quickly came down from the horse behind them, putting a hand on the duke's shoulder to restrain him.

"Do not lose your temper now, My Lord," he said. "We must keep moving. Let the village and I handle this and the king handle your son."

His words, however, fell on deaf ears, the duke seemingly entranced as he stared into Luna's eyes.

Suddenly, Caedon screamed, "Nooooo!"

The duke's whip hit the horse's hindquarters and the cart lurched forward, bringing Luna tumbling to the ground hard as she frantically clawed at the rope around her neck. It was only about 10 feet, but damage had been done as the priest brought the spooked horse to a halt.

The duchess was completely aghast, as Caedon barreled out of his cart, having lunged several times into the door, splitting the wood around the lock. With lightning reflex, Caedon brought his tied hands overtop his father's head in one swift motion, pulling the rope tight against his throat.

Horrified, the duke struggled to find air. The magistrate came at them both, but Caedon tightened the rope in response, causing Duke Nicolai to wave off his would-be rescuer.

As a result, Caedon loosened his grip slightly, his eyes darting between the magistrate, the armed guards and the priest, who was untying an unconscious Luna.

Finally, he met Duchess Rosalind's eyes and held them.

What she saw ignited tears, her arms falling to her sides in defeat. She rolled her eyes up to the stars, then let them rest on Luna's tattered form before looking down at her feet in shame.

Gaining composure, the duchess hoisted herself back onto her horse, gave Caedon one more long gaze, before riding off into the woods, enveloped by the trees' black shadows.

*****

Caedon turned his attention back to his father, now growing lethargic from the lack of oxygen to his brain.

"If you ever touch her again, I *will* kill you ... just like you and Darius killed mother."

The statement was made for only the duke's ears, but both the magistrate and priest watched his face warp into one of unadulterated terror.

Two guards rushed Caedon, as his father slumped to the ground, free of his son's grasp. Caedon strained to look back at Luna, making sure she was coherent, making sure she was alive. To his dismay, he only caught a glimpse of her toes before he was thrown into the back of the cart, now tied at his legs as well.

The priest lifted Luna into his arms, desperately trying to desensitize himself to the feeling of her pressed against him as he laid her unconscious body back into the carriage.

He immediately wished to scrub himself raw from her scent, her blood, her skin. He locked the door and got back into the front of the cart, driving the horse forward.

*****

Luna woke up to the clank of metal on metal. She looked around, seeing she was in a cell, yet it was clearly not the prison in her village.

Baffled, she smelled the air, catching a strong scent of mint, cloves and boot wax. She sat up slowly, her muscles aching as she racked her brain to remember what happened.

She looked down at her body, seeing dried blood caked to her legs and elbows, and feeling it stiff at her throat. She remembered the sound of the whip. Closing out the memory, Luna shut her eyes tightly, before hearing a stir.

She opened them to Duke Nicolai, standing on the other side of the iron bars before her. He had bathed and dressed, and she realized the scent of mint, cloves and shoe polish belonged to him. She wanted to vomit.

"I must ... apologize. You see, the last woman to stir emotions such as those, was my ... was my late wife," the duke said, as though he and Luna were old friends. She quickly wondered where Caedon was. She couldn't sense him.

Reading her thoughts, the duke slowly shook his head and smiled.

"He's being held elsewhere, far from the reaches of your guiles, your spells."

"I am not what you say I am," Luna said simply, making sure to keep her breath even. "I am just a woman who fell in love with a man. Your son."

The duke seemed to mull over her words, tasting them, before cringing with disgust.

"You are a filthy little liar. You are your mother's child. Yes, I knew of your mother. I knew of her dealings with *my* wife," he said, practically choking on the words.

Luna's mind reeled at his admittance.

"It was your mother who hexed my wife, who tainted her. Lucinda would speak of ludicrous things, but they were musings put into her mind by *your* mother," he said, keeping his tone controlled. "And Darius, she continued to neglect him, to put him off on the servants. I had no time for him then and it pains me to say so, but it was her duty to care for him!"

Silence filled the air as Luna waited for him to regain himself.

"Lucinda grew ... unstable, was beginning to speak of heresy. I would not allow it in my house, under my rule. I would not allow my family to be shamed in such a way."

"So you killed her," Luna said.

The duke paused, shifting his weight to the other foot as he took a step closer to the bars separating them.

"You killed her by slowly poisoning her, yet you made Darius an unwitting accomplice, giving him the glass or food to take to her every time," Luna whispered. "Leading Caedon to question his own brother and planting an even darker seed in Darius' conscience once he discovered what he had been a part of. I could only assume you told him."

"Darius always knew, on some level. He was already lost, mentally. Lucinda lost him. She allowed him to slip away day by day, while doting on Caedon."

"As did you," Luna countered, halting the duke momentarily.

"Yes, I did, but only because I had to groom an heir and Darius was clearly out of the question."

"You convinced that poor child that by unknowingly killing his mother, he had rid the world of a great evil!" Luna snarled. "He may have been saved, but you sealed his fate in that moment."

The duke violently shook his head, stepping right up against the metal and causing Luna to fight the urge to step back. Instead, she stepped forward, bringing them within a foot of each other.

His breath smelled of cheese and wine, acrid, just as his youngest son's had been. Luna's stomach curled, but she held still.

"Darius was meant to do what he did. He was born to do what he did. Just as Lucinda was fated to die the moment she met with your wicked mother. And just as Caedon was born to be my heir – until you entered his life. Your mother's final curse on our family nearly fulfilled."

The words stung, yet Luna remained solemn, her eyes beginning to swirl with unsolicited emotion.

"My mother met with your wife at *her* request. There was nothing evil about either of them. They asked questions, they thought past the scriptures, and for that, they're heretics? Wicked? They had *good* hearts. They were *good* women and it was sadistic obsessions and twisted, morbid beliefs such as yours that doomed them!"

The duke's hand shot out. Luna, tied up, was helpless to react. His fingers closed around her neck, pressing against the rope burns on her throat. Her eyes brimmed with hot tears as she gasped for breath. Lifting her knee, she kicked out, making contact with the duke's kneecap and feeling a satisfying crunch beneath her heal.

He released her, the momentum causing her to fly backward and land hard on the cold stone floor. The duke wailed in pain, folding over while grabbing his knee. Guards immediately stormed in, helping him out of the room while unlocking her cell. She was grabbed, pulled from the room and bent over a chair in one fluid motion.

Closing her eyes, she awaited the first strike.

Sure enough, it came.

The stiff leather strap felt as though it had never been broken in. Every hit left a sharp burn in its wake, slicing into her skin. She awaited the fire inside of her to take hold. But something else – perhaps the part of her craving punishment for the role she played in her and Caedon's demise – reigned over her instead.

Eventually, Luna felt nothing, a numbness that froze her bones. She tried to fight it, but blackness tore at the corners of her vision, eventually consuming her.

Releasing a long breath, she fell limp against the chair.

Chapter 27

The sharp clank of metal startled Luna awake. She realized she was cloaked in darkness and in a different cell. The floor felt gritty beneath her shoulder as she noticed she had been laid on her side. Momentarily forgetting why, she wiggled onto her back and cried out in agony. It felt as though a thousand hornets had ravished her shoulder blades.

She heard another clamor near her and squinted toward the noise, seeing a dim candle flickering in the corner of the room. Finally, she heard voices, muffled by the stone walls surrounding her, but drawing nearer. A sudden gust of humid, oppressive air hit her as a door flew open, stealing her breath. The doorframe flooded with light and Luna's pupils struggled to adjust. Between the bars, she saw a towering silhouette.

Perhaps it was lack of sleep and sustenance, or the pain still tingling on the fringes of her consciousness, but for a split second, Luna saw Darius' cold, torrential eyes staring back at her.

As the figure stepped forward, Darius' ghost of a face faded and was filled, instead, by a very solemn, very turgid and more importantly, very *real* village magistrate.

"Hello, Luna Fortella, daughter of Jevan and Cybele Fortella," he said in a cracked voice, scarred by years of pipe smoke.

The use of her surname stunned Luna. The last time it was uttered was during the reading of her mother's last rites.

"I am Tobias Avery," he said in an eerily hushed tenor. "King Bertrem has requested your presence and I am to deliver you to him."

Luna tried to hide her consternation by swallowing it down like a rancid grape, yet the bitterness remained pungent in her mouth as she slowly exhaled.

"I will not touch you, not even to help you up, but I suggest you get up soon or the guards will make you stand themselves," he said frostily.

While his seeming disdain for her dusted every syllable, she felt an ounce of gratitude for his warning. He could have very well said nothing and let the guards grab her up without a thought to her wounded back and battered limbs.

She rolled onto her side, wincing at the pain of her skin splitting open. Biting her lip, she closed her eyes and pushed off her right shoulder, sitting up and placing her tied wrists in her lap for a second to absorb the pain. Faint footsteps of approaching guards gave her all the momentum she needed to rise to her feet.

"Now, step forward with your eyes to the floor and your arms down at all times," Tobias said.

Luna could not place it, but something about his voice, his demeanor spurred an instinct to comply without question. It both disturbed and intrigued her as she stepped forward as commanded.

With slow deliberation, Tobias unlocked the cell door, his eyes never leaving Luna's face yet never meeting her downcast lashes.

"I once knew your father and mother well," he whispered.

The words stung Luna, yet she was careful not to look up at him, nor speak, even though curiosity burned against her lips. Much to her relief, he continued.

"Your father and I were boyhood friends. I was there when he met your mother," he said.

Luna's mind struggled to comprehend his words as the guards' footfalls drew nearer.

"She was dancing. It was quite alluring," he said. "I could not blame him for his immediate attraction to Cybele. She was immensely captivating."

As he recalled the event, his voice grew momentarily soft. However, it was fleeting and icy shadows returned as he resumed the tale.

"I warned your father against her, telling him she was ... unnatural," he said. "But he did not listen. He had fallen for her in a breath's moment and there was nothing I could do or say to convince him otherwise. Yet, they managed to quiet the village chatter over time, so I decided to give them the benefit of the doubt. They invited me over many times for dinner before they had you. I was grateful as I had to care for my ailing mother on very little salary and the free meals were a relief. But after my mother passed, I decided to leave the village and start a new life. It was not until I saw your father again, in my village, that I heard of what had happened. I promised him I would keep the secret of your mother's execution as long as neither he, nor you, nor anyone in your household caused me any trouble."

Astonished her father never divulged such information to her over the years, especially on his deathbed, Luna stood there with her mouth agape as she stared at the floor.

"However, now it seems a whole whirlwind of trouble has been stirred, not just in my village, but at the king's estate as well – and all of it by you," Tobias said. "Unfortunately, dear Luna, I do not have any more breaks to give."

His words sliced through her like a fine butcher knife splitting the skin of an apple. In that moment, the guards arrived, standing like statues by the doorway as Tobias somberly stepped aside to let Luna pass through.

She shuffled forward, suppressing the urge to whimper with each movement, which brought the sting of air against her wounds. She could only imagine how broken, disheveled and unkempt she must look, but her spirit was beyond reticent, so she shambled down the long corridor ahead of her.

As she began climbing a stone stairway leading to more familiar surroundings, her legs atrophied, sending her to the ground. But before she hit, a strong, steady hand caught her arm, holding her up.

She turned her head to meet Tobias' eyes for the first time. They were a light hazel color. He did not break her gaze, but he also held caution in his stare. Luna brought her guard down, let him in and watched his stony face transform to the very same softness he wore when he first spoke of her mother. It was brief, but the meaningful exchange felt necessary.

Regaining composure, Luna made her way up the rest of the stairs, through several wings of the castle she had never visited and finally into the king's court. Just as she began crossing the threshold, one of the guards tripped her with his walking stick, sending her careening to the floor.

The motion caused every nerve in Luna's body to scream, yet she held quiet and still, bowing her head, ashamed of her appearance.

Then, she looked up and saw King Bertrem's glorious figure, seated in the center of the room.

Unlike her last encounter with His Majesty, this time, his eyes fixed on no one else but her.

Chapter 28

The king's scrutinizing gaze held Luna prisoner. She cast her eyes to the marble floor, focusing on the ebb and flow of its swirling design. The airy, expansive room – filled with at least a hundred members of the king's court – fell silent, though hushed whispers grazed Luna's ears like a soft breeze through blades of grass. After several crawling moments, the king's furrowed brow and sharp glare softened slightly, causing a stir in the room. His eyes moved to the duke, who was standing adjacent to him and deliberately keeping his focus away from Luna's direction.

The king huffed, catching the duke's attention.

"This is it? This ragged, sullied, wayward excuse for a servant girl is what has an entire village on the edge of panic, has interrupted vital peace negotiations, disturbed my entire kingdom and put my longtime confidant, Duke Nicolai, in very rare form?" he bellowed, his voice echoing off the walls, causing Luna to wince.

The duke finally looked at Luna. She unconsciously clenched her fists as her eyes continued to bore into the stone slab beneath her.

"You mean to tell me that this tattered, weary girl before me was capable of murdering *your* son?"

The duke's eyes shot back to the king, revealing a rare display of intimidation.

"She is not what she seems, Your Excellency," he whispered, before dropping his eyes to the floor. Luna realized then just how feared and respected King Bertrem truly was, which added a fresh layer of trepidation to her nerves.

After studying the duke a moment longer, the king returned his gaze to Luna, who was careful to keep her own eyes lowered.

"Step forward, girl."

Tobias notably cleared his throat, which pushed Luna unsteadily to her feet. She kept her head bowed as she hesitantly shuffled toward the king, stopping at the end of the burgundy rug a few feet from his elevated throne. A breeze from the nearby window brushed past the king, carrying a heavy scent of citrus and pipe smoke to Luna's nose.

"Look at me."

She complied, raising her eyes to meet his sturdy gaze. His brow furrowed once more as he studied her. She felt her skin lightly tingle under his penetrating stare, the tension almost too much to bear. Suddenly, his steady breath caught ever so slightly. No one heard it, except Luna, yet it was not his breath that grabbed her attention. It was the brief change in his eyes, revealing a fleeting emotion resembling timidity. Luna held her breath then, begging the king to release her gaze. A glimpse of disbelief washed over his face before he finally tore his eyes from hers.

"You may return to Tobias," he said gruffly, loudly shifting on his throne.

"What evidence do you have against this girl?"

Tobias stepped forward, bowing slightly before solemnly facing the king.

"Following the discovery of an old vagrant man's body in the woods not far from my village, a torn piece of cloth was found on him," Tobias said. "We have since linked it to a blouse found in a trunk owned by the girl in question."

King Bertrem simply nodded.

"Duke Nicolai's ... late son, Darius –" Tobias said, glancing briefly at the duke, who remained stone-faced, "told me recently of an altercation he had with the girl in your stables, indicating she had attacked him. Duchess Rosalind confirmed."

"And you have reason to believe a woman of her size could overpower someone like Darius?" the king asked, skepticism dripping from every syllable.

The duke winced and puckered his lips, fighting back words.

Tobias mulled over the question.

"I am not sure," he finally muttered.

The duke let out an exasperated breath but held still when the king glared at him.

"Continue," the king said after a moment longer.

"The day of Darius' murder, the girl was said to have gone to the stables to perform her daily chores," Tobias said, glancing to the left corner of the room. Luna's eyes followed, landing on Katrin. Her face was expressionless, but her eyes betrayed a mixture of sadness, fear and doubt. Luna's heart twisted into knots beneath her ribs as she returned her eyes to the trim on Tobias' robe.

"Darius was seen going into the stables not long after," Tobias said. "This was reported by the same servant."

The king only glanced at Katrin briefly before looking back at Tobias.

"According to my reports, no one seemed to have heard the altercation. However, the duke's other son, Caedon, entered the stables shortly thereafter as well," Tobias said, giving a slight nod in Katrin's direction.

The king, now deep in thought, only nodded back, running his tongue along his upper teeth through pursed lips.

"What happened after can only be concluded by the disappearance of Caedon, his horse and the girl, as well as where they were all found – at the late queen's cabin."

This, above all other factors, seemed to affect the king the most. Luna realized in that moment not only the depth of King Bertrem's love for his late queen, but the grave insult their presence in the cabin had been. She swallowed, tasting blood at the back of her parched throat.

Though the king remained level, the muscles along his jawline twitched.

"Your Highness' bloodhounds have since discovered the dagger. Duchess Rosalind found the girl's tattered clothes covered in what we can only assume is Darius' blood," Tobias said. "And what's more, Father Hans has confirmed the girl is the daughter of a woman who was condemned for witchcraft and burned at the stake many years ago."

His last words seemed to pour from his lips at the pace of

molasses. Luna clenched her hands into fists beside her bent knee and squeezed her eyelids shut against her mother's memory.

This last part made the king sit up straighter as his eyes landed on Luna for the first time since he had dismissed her. The mention of his cabin pushed to the fringes of his thoughts as he weighed Tobias' implications.

"Are you insinuating this girl somehow shares the same ... sacrilege her mother did?"

Tobias' eyes also fell onto Luna, who now kneeled on both legs, wishing she could melt into the floor.

"It has been ... suggested," he said cautiously.

The king sat back, the wood creaking beneath his weight as he brought his chin to rest on his palm.

"Because you realize, Tobias, such fears and anxieties have ebbed a great deal in recent years. Furthermore, threats of blasphemy and witchcraft are rarely handled in such a manner anymore," the king said.

Tobias nodded, but kept his mouth shut, everyone's eyes remaining on the king.

"Murder, however, is quite a different matter," he said, stroking his jaw before shaking his head as if in a trance. He brought his attention back to Tobias.

"Your Majesty, in examining the body and the wound, the blade seems to have entered at an angle that indicates either a very intentional close range, upward thrust ... or accidental penetration," Tobias said, causing a wave of gasps throughout the room.

"Are you suggesting that my son ran into a blade held by that whore on accident?" the duke growled.

"Nicolai! Remember yourself," the king snapped, causing the duke to slink backward, bowing his head in shame.

"I think we can safely rule that out," King Bertrem said calmly.

"Admittedly, the probability would be low," Tobias concurred.

Luna bit down on her tongue so hard, she half expected the bitter, metallic taste of blood to ensue.

"Then it is to be concluded, based on all the evidence, that there was an altercation between the girl, Darius and Caedon," the king said. "Who spurred it is still unknown, but at some point, a dagger was drawn by either Darius or Caedon, as it has Duke Nicolai's initials engraved on the handle. Yes?"

Tobias nodded solemnly, shifting his weight from his left leg to his right. Luna could practically smell the oiled leather of his boots. Feeling nauseous, she suppressed the urge to gag while trying to remain steady as the edges of her vision wavered.

"At some point, however, the girl got a hold of the dagger and stabbed Darius at close range," the king finished. "What of the notion of self-defense?"

Tobias slowly shook his head.

"We are just not sure, Your Highness," he said. "But, given the mysterious circumstances surrounding the death of the man in the woods, which has been evidentially linked to her; the history of her family; and the eye-witness testimony surrounding Darius' first altercation with the girl, as well as his death, an overwhelming number of factors indicate an intentional stabbing."

The room burst with raucous chatter. Luna's strength gave in, sending her crashing to the floor. Tobias grabbed her arm before her forehead hit the marble, as one of the other guards moved forward to help him.

"Liars!" a voice thundered against the walls, evoking a sharp hush. Everyone, including the king himself, was jarred by the sound, as all eyes turned to the back of the room.

A silhouette stepped into the candlelight, revealing irises blazing with rage. Slowly coming to, Luna squinted at the figure until her eyes reached his.

She would know them anywhere.

Chapter 29

Caedon shuffled forward, disobeying the chains around his ankles and wrists. Two guards bumbled in behind him, out of breath and apologetic in their bows to the king.

"What is the meaning of this intrusion?" King Bertrem asked demandingly.

"Your Excellency, I apologize. After you had asked that we bring in Caedon, he managed to ... briefly evade us during the transition," one of the guards confessed, mortified.

"I am not running a fools festival. From now on, my own guards will deal with any transfer of prisoners. You two may retire to your village," the king said.

Two soldiers moved forward from the doors, quickly taking the place of the chagrined guards.

The king's gaze settled on Caedon, who briefly bowed before meeting his stare. Unlike his father, Caedon never flinched, even as the king's eyes burned into him, studying every emotion passing over his face.

"Caedon, I have known you your entire life. I reveled in the glow of your mother's face when she carried you. I was there when your father first brought you to my home, swaddled in the blue blanket my ... late wife had made for you. She could not wait to have a child like you," the king said, revealing a flash of cutting despair before returning Caedon's stony glare.

"And here you stand, the heir to your father's estate, title and land – and now a suspect in the murder of your own brother," King Bertrem said, his brow creased with tension and disappointment.

Caedon never relinquished his gaze, however, he swallowed slowly, his jaw twitching through clenched teeth.

"Your father accuses you of being bewitched by this servant girl. Darius made similar statements prior to his death. In addition, you were clearly involved in his murder as you were seen entering the stables before his death. If all these things are true, you have betrayed your family, your honor, God's will and your kingdom," the king said, his hands gripping the edges of his wooden armrests as he slid slightly forward in his throne.

"And despite all of this, you have the audacity to storm through my doors and call everyone in this room a liar, including myself."

Caedon looked to the floor, giving King Bertrem what he was looking for. He settled back into his chair and brought his fingertips together in front of his chest, studying Luna briefly, before looking back at Caedon.

"Explain your accusation."

At this, Caedon looked through the corners of his eyes at Luna, still kneeling on the floor, hiding behind tousled tresses of raven hair. Seeing her appearance, his expression softened for an instant before hardening under the king's stare.

"Luna did not intentionally stab Darius. He attacked her and I walked in during the conflict. The stabbing was an accident."

"He's mad! My poor son has lost his mind," Duke Nicolai cried out, causing another caustic glare from the king.

"Let him speak," he said, returning his attention back to Caedon.

"I came to her defense, and during the altercation, he went after her with the dagger. She did the only thing she could. She turned it on him," Caedon said, flinching at the memory.

"But evidence indicates the speed at which such an action would have to occur is near impossible. And, even if it did happen as you say it did, other collected evidence points to an intentional stabbing," the king replied.

"It does not completely rule out self-defense," Caedon countered.

The king rolled his tongue around his mouth, pondering Caedon's words. He looked at the duke's pleading eyes, then at Tobias, before turning his eyes toward Luna.

"Stand up, girl," he said.

Luna fumbled to her feet, bringing her eyes to meet the king's. He turned to look at Caedon.

"While I do not understand the *hold* this girl has on you, and apparently had on your brother, I do understand infatuation and irrational attachment," the king said. "At one time, Caedon, your word would hold weight in my kingdom and in my eyes. But much has happened in the recent months to make me question your integrity, your loyalty."

The latter statement caused Caedon to catch his breath, remembering similar words spoken by the king to his brother before sentencing him to death for suspected treason. Knowing he was treading on very thin ice, he decided it was now or never.

"You question *my* loyalty? Ask my father the true nature of my mother's death!" Caedon growled.

Taken aback by his outburst, the king's eyes widened, momentarily befuddled by his words.

"Nicolai?" the king said, raising his eyebrows at the duke.

"I've already told you, Your Majesty. He is unstable, he's lost his sanity," the duke said. "I fear I have not lost just one son, but both."

"You lie," Caedon seethed, edging forward despite the tight grips of the soldiers at his sides.

"I have proof. My mother's journal – "

"Your mother was ill, Caedon. In those last weeks, she did not know what was real and what was a delusion," the duke said, feigning pity and compassion.

"She was lucid, father. She had been well aware of the fact you had Darius slowly poisoning her because of your ludicrous belief she was a heathen. You infected my brother's mind with your own twisted judgment and paranoia. I have the pages she wrote in. I was there, I remember my brother taking her tea and meals from your den. You had the servants deliver her meals to you first," Caedon said, his eyes glistening.

The king's eyes bore into him, gauging his sincerity.

"Your Highness, you've known me all these years. You know how I adored my wife," the duke said, his voice teetering beneath his words.

King Bertrem studied him, then Caedon.

"Nicolai, yes, I have known you many years. I knew your wife.

She was a very dear friend to my own," he said, pausing for several moments. "When she was getting worse, there was one evening in which she confided to the late queen she felt unsafe with you. I, of course, chose to overlook such a statement, taking into consideration her condition and giving you the benefit of the doubt. But with your own son, who, as far as I can tell, is of complete sound mind, telling me the like and possessing evidence of it, I am not so certain anymore."

"Your Majesty, you cannot possibly – "

The king's hand flew up, staying the duke's words.

"I am not finished."

The duke bent his head in response.

"The person before me is a stranger. I hardly recognize him," he continued, referring to Duke Nicolai. "My instincts tell me that something very dark and ugly has transpired in this family. Whether it is this recent tragedy or something that goes back much further, as I fear it does, it fills me with the greatest remorse."

His words, uncommonly raw, sent shivers through the duke.

The king turned his attention to Luna, who had struggled to her feet, despite knees weakened by sleep deprivation and shredded nerves.

"And what have you to say about this?"

Luna's eyes, a mixture of charcoal and silvery hues, met the king's. She felt Caedon's gaze upon her, nearly causing her sudden burst of courage to falter.

"I saw the pages of which Caedon speaks."

"No. I'm referring to his statements about what happened in that barn, on *my* peaceful grounds and on *my* land."

Luna hesitated, but found her voice quickly.

"That is the way of it," she said simply.

"I see," he replied, before looking at Tobias and then the duke. "I will look over the evidence that has been presented to me, as well as the statements made in this very room tonight. Tomorrow, I will declare my ruling."

The duke loudly exhaled as Luna began to sink to the floor.

Caedon strained to move in her direction but was held still by the guards. Tobias, however, clutched her arm and moved her toward the doors and out of Caedon's sight.

She turned her head, desperate to catch a glimpse of him. Tobias sternly pulled her forward as everyone slowly filtered from the room. She pulled backward against the crowd, struggling to see Caedon, if only for a moment. Just as the doors began to close behind her, she caught a glimpse of his eyes, scouring for hers.

They bled tears.

Chapter 30

The hours seemed to melt together as Luna awaited the king's decision. She was thrown back into her cell. Though this time, she was given a vat of lukewarm water, soap and a brush to wash herself.

Feeling the layers of grit and dried blood on her skin, she could not wait to cleanse her body of these haunting reminders. However, she also desired to bask in their rawness and pain, to let them emanate the torment she endured.

The brush's coarse bristles sliced into her skin, making her wince with every stroke. She held her breath as she scrubbed her hands, wrists and arms. Trembling from the sting, she gingerly put the brush down beside her knees and brought two handfuls of water to her face and neck. The soap seared her wounds. She decided against washing the rope burns around her neck, despite a feverish itch caused by caked blood. Instead, she delicately tended to the other parts of her body, mindful of the guards near the door. Tobias had disappeared once she was taken back into the king's custody. She assumed he would not return until summoned again. Much to her relief, Duke Nicolai never came back to her cell. Luna recalled the wave of satisfaction she had felt in his aberrant fear of King Bertrem.

However, she dared not allow her thoughts to venture in the direction of a pair of cobalt eyes filled with anguish. For if she did, the last shred of fortitude pulsing faintly through her veins would dissolve.

Instead, she thought back on Tobias' words to her before he led her into the king's court. How, despite this revealed history with her parents, he was powerless to aid her. She thought of her mother. How Luna ached for her in these moments, for her soft touch, for the way she used to ardently move Luna's hair from her eyes and hold her jutted chin in her hand. The way she had smelled faintly of vanilla and honeysuckle, and when Luna would hug her, she'd breathe her in so deep. The way the sunlight played on the specks of gold in her mother's eyes and how they would glow when she looked at her husband.

Luna let her thoughts graze over the memory of her father, his gentle spirit and peaceful disposition, how he balanced out her mother's fiery temper and zealous nature, and how both flowed through Luna's veins. The memories, though glazed with melancholy, brought Luna a sense of solace she had not felt since she was last enveloped in Caedon's arms.

A desolate sigh escaped her lips as she dried her skin and curled up on the cold floor. Sleep did not come easily, but eventually, it arrived.

*****

The sharp clank of metal yanked Luna from a dreamless slumber. She swiftly sat up and hugged her knees to her chest as a guard opened her cell door. He stepped forward with an outstretched hand, though he was careful not to meet her eyes. Before she could help herself, Luna smirked in amusement. Here she was, her wits barely intact, yet this hulking man was timorous.

Hiding her face behind the locks of hair cascading down her shoulders, Luna stood and stepped toward the guard, avoiding his arm. He grabbed onto her shoulder and shoved her forward while another guard held the door open before leading the way back to the king's court.

Once again, Tobias greeted Luna, only his expression seemed colder than before. Yet, the briefest of emotion swept passed his eyes as he held out his hand.

"I believe this is yours."

Luna looked down and gasped. It was her mother's scarf.

Holding back tears, she quickly pulled her hair back with it, softly cleared her throat and moved past Tobias into the same room she was in the prior evening. However, this time it was filled with even more members of the king's court, as well as their acquaintances. Luna wanted to shrink into the wall behind her, but instead, she swallowed her anxiety and stepped forward to bow before the king.

Another door opened at the rear of the room. Luna turned her head sideways to see Duke Nicolai enter, followed by Caedon, who appeared to have been washed and given a fresh change of clothing. The king studied all three of them, allowing his eyes to take Luna in slightly longer. Although she was still wearing tattered clothes that barely hid her wounds and bruised neck, her hair had been washed and tied back, revealing cleansed skin and a brighter complexion. The king seemed to catch a fleeting glimpse of what had drawn Darius and Caedon to her, yet he did not linger on it. His business had been interrupted by the current state of affairs long enough.

"Caedon, step forward."

Moving around his father, Caedon complied, bowing to the king before meeting his eyes.

"Your Highness," he said steadily, though Luna caught a hint of trepidation in his voice.

"In reviewing your statement, the evidence at hand, as well as witness statements, I cannot condemn you to death, though you clearly had part in your brother's demise and what transpired in its wake."

While the king could not bring himself to outwardly acknowledge Caedon had taken Luna to his late wife's private cabin, the implication of it weighed heavily. Caedon simply held his breath, waiting for the ensuing words.

"For those reasons, you have betrayed not only our Lord, my kingdom, your country and your family, but you have betrayed yourself," the king said.

Every word must have felt like a separate anvil being lowered on Caedon's chest, yet he kept his gaze sturdy.

"Therefore, I am forced to take away your inheritance, strip you of your title and condemn you to my prison for the next decade and a half of your life, without pardon. However, I will allow certain liberties as I see fit," he said.

Caedon's eyes fell to the floor, his hands tightening beside him. A single tear broke free, trickling down his cheek before falling to the floor. Luna brought her face to her hands, unable to maintain her resolve any longer. She shook with waves of tribulation. The king squinted as he studied her reaction, slightly surprised by its intensity. The moment was brief as the turgid movement of the guards brought his attention back to Caedon.

He had no fight in him this time, as he was quietly led into the shadows of the back corner. The king turned his focus on Duke Nicolai. The duke averted his eyes to the king's feet as he bowed ever so slightly and stepped forward.

"Nicolai," King Bertrem said, pausing to collect his thoughts. Luna noticed a slight struggle in his eyes.

"I find myself torn in several directions. While I lost my firstborn son to war, it did not ebb the immense sorrow a parent feels when losing a child, regardless of the circumstances. And to lose a wife ..."

Once more, the king betrayed a sliver of rarely displayed emotion before quickly gathering himself.

"So, you could imagine my complete bewilderment when I read the haunting things exposed in the pages of your late wife's journal," King Bertrem said. "They were written well before her illness took full effect on her lucidity, Nicolai."

His words pierced any retort the duke had planned. Instead, he shrunk back.

"Furthermore, your son, who, despite his crimes and betrayals, continues to appear to be of sound mind – his statements coincide with Lucinda's writings," the king said. "I am aware of this servant girl's mother's history, as well as her ties to Lucinda. I am aware of Father Geirnuk's opinion on that history, as well as this girl. I have also taken into account the village magistrate's statements on both. While I know such blasphemy exists in the world and has been condemned by harsh means on our own lands for many years, and while I know such evil could very well have influenced your sons to such actions, I have enough information before me to infer that this darkness goes back much further than this girl before me. And while evidence is meager in that regard, I am gravely sickened that such twisted secrecy has been within my walls for all these years, at my right-hand side, breathing the same air I breathe."

Perhaps it was merely the tension preying on his nerves or the cutting disgust in the king's tone, but the duke's fingers began to quiver as he bent his head farther down, never once looking at the king with the same courage his son mustered.

"Nicolai, you've known me many years. I have done so much for you, your late wife and your sons. You have worked with me by my side, witnessed predicaments I have been put in, the trials I've endured and the punishments I have had to mete. Yet here you are, lying in my very presence about what has truly transpired – as if you do not know just how cunning my detection of dishonesty can be."

The duke continued to bow in silence, realizing nothing he said now would hold any bearing on the king's decision.

"However, because of the years you dedicated to the positive cause of peace between our lands and people, and because I do not have enough evidence to, in good faith, convict you entirely of the atrocities that have been suggested, I will condemn you in a different way."

The entire room seemed to hold its breath as King Bertrem allowed several moments to pass before he continued.

"You will forthwith be stripped of your title, your inheritance and your land, and you will be banished from these lands for the rest of your days. If you so much as set one foot in this kingdom again, you will be executed, without exception," the king said, holding his voice steady, despite the ire lacing every syllable.

The duke, finally overcome, fell to his knees. Three guards instantly stepped forward to lift his limp form off the floor and out of the room.

Luna exhaled, as did the rest of the room. She searched for Caedon's eyes, hidden in the shadows adjacent to her. She felt them on her. In that moment, relief washed over her, as well as a sense of atonement for Lucinda – and even Darius, who never had the chance to witness it.

However, the feeling was fleeting, as Luna realized her fate loomed. Caedon, arriving at this same conclusion, stood in the darkness, his eyes piercing with mixed emotion.

The king, regaining himself after the duke's departure, continued on.

"Luna Fortella," the king said. The sound of her full name on his lips stilled her heart and froze her limbs.

"Stand up and step forward."

A few moments passed. The guards, quickly losing their patience, began to move forward, but were stayed by the king's subtle lift of a finger.

He waited.

Feeling the pulse of her heart throbbing against her ears, Luna forced herself to her feet.

The silence continued as she kept her eyes affixed to the floor beneath her. But she knew that would not do. She knew what he was waiting for.

After what seemed an eternity, Luna reached deep down inside herself and found her mother's eyes. Her body began to fill with an energy not entirely her own.

She took a deep breath, took another step forward and lifted her head.

Then, as sharp as a whip to a horse, her gaze locked onto King Bertrem's. He inhaled through his teeth.

Her eyes were black as coal. And flames danced in them.

Chapter 31

The king swallowed his bewilderment and cleared his throat. His eyes remained steadily on Luna's, despite the chill scampering down each of his vertebrae. There was something in her that left him unsettled, something mystical yet strong and pure – and rarely seen in those who stood before him in court. Through the night, as he weighed her punishment, he'd wrestled with this unfamiliar dynamic – an internal struggle he intended to free himself of in levying his sentence.

"I have found myself, admittedly, in foreign territory," King Bertrem said. "I have reviewed your family history, these multiple firsthand accounts of an unnatural allure you allegedly have, evidence pointing to your involvement in an altercation that spurred the death of an elderly man in the woods, and the evidence and witness testimonies regarding your most recent encounters with Darius and Caedon. I have also taken into account input from your household staff and your closest remaining kin – your cousin, Melvan – which did you some credit. However, with the evidence drawn by Magistrate Tobias Avery, though not entirely proven, my hands are quite tied. During my father's time, he would have instantly condemned you to death, not only for your involvement in the death of a nobleman, but also for the sacrilegious implications made by members of my court, my priest and members of your village –"

"No one beyond my household knows anything of me!" Luna snapped, her eyes piercing.

The king shot up from his throne. The motion caused gasps about the room as, in a giant wave, the entire court knelt to the floor.

All except Luna.

Fists clenched at his sides, the king towered over her turgid figure, an earnest outward display of authority that concealed his internal uneasiness toward her. The guards began to step forward when his hand flew up to halt them. His eyes bore into hers as they both held their stance.

Eventually, the king's hands went lax as he took several deep breaths, never breaking their stare. Luna exhaled steadily, her body and hard expression unwavering.

"You will ... watch that insubordinate mouth of yours," the king gruffly replied.

Luna said nothing. However, her dark eyes finally broke away. After a few moments, the king was satisfied enough to return to his throne.

"As I was saying, during my father's time, these allegations would be met with death. However, as everyone knows, our laws have progressed from those ... more barbaric forms of punishment. So, I have decided to stray from precedent. I am sentencing you to life in prison," the king said, causing incredulous cries from the court.

"Quiet!" he thundered, bringing instant silence. "I am not finished. This decree is contingent on and subordinate to your village's judgment."

Whispers of confusion swarmed around the room. Years of ruling his kingdom and peace talks had taught King Bertram what many in the room couldn't fully grasp: how to strategize. He wanted to distance himself from the savage punishments of past generations and rule in a more civilized manner, but he also knew his people would demand justice – and perhaps question his rule if he did not deliver. His savvy plan was to issue a harsh but just sentence while allowing others to ultimately decide, thus washing his hands of the matter and allowing him to return to what he deemed more important: negotiating treaties.

The king patiently waited for their drones to abate.

"In short, Luna Fortella, I am turning your fate to the people of your village."

*****

The walls closed in on Luna, smothering her. She must have fainted, her lungs screeching for air as she shook King Bertrem's words from her mind and inhaled a jagged breath.

She had been transported to another prison cell, one that made her almost long for the former.

The ground was stained crimson from rust that bled into its cracks with each heavy rainfall. The bars were chipped and caked with years of grime and human filth. Luna hugged her knees and slowly began to rock in place.

It was not long before a gust of dank air whipped past her nose, bringing her attention to the jangling keys and shuffling feet gradually advancing.

Luna's eyes squinted into the dimly lit room, quickly realizing there was not just one person approaching her cell, there were three.

Tobias, Dirdra and Regan.

Sweetest Dirdra, always something baked in her arms, removed the cloth from a round loaf of sweet bread, releasing its buttery aroma and engulfing Luna's senses. She hadn't realized until that moment how famished she was.

Luna sluggishly stood, ambling to the bars to receive the loaf. As she did, Dirdra touched her knuckles softly, giving Luna's fingers a squeeze before releasing them and bringing the cloth to her brimming eyes.

She sniffled, instantly reminding Luna this was not the first time she faced losing someone she dearly loved in their household. Regan appeared more composed, albeit tense with anxiety. It was then Luna realized Regan was slightly afraid of her. Not so much of Luna herself, but of what coming there in support of her might do to both Dirdra and herself, and to what's left of the estate.

Luna took a large bite of the warm, flaky bread, using every ounce of self-control she had left to keep from gorging the entire thing. Regan, sensing her parched throat, extended a cup of water that had been concealed by the shadows.

Perhaps it was hours of hunger, the lack of sleep or maybe she had gone slightly mad, but it was that simple deed that broke Luna's staunch resolve. She shook with misery, hunching over the bread while leaning into the bars and awkward embraces from Dirdra and

Regan. Tobias remained stiff several feet back, though he patiently allowed the exchange.

After several moments, Luna pulled back and brought her lips to the wooden cup, giving herself a moment to enjoy the electric rush of cool water slide down her throat and sink into her stomach the way she used to as a child. Her mind was grasping for a sense of normalcy within a tempest of confusion.

"Dirdra, I– " she began, but faltered. Dirdra wiped Luna's eyes and softly hushed her.

"Say nothing, Miss Luna. There is nothing you need to say to me. Just as there was nothing your mother or father needed to say," she whispered.

Luna only nodded, overcome with a gamut of emotions she could not readily place, let alone rein in.

She then turned to Regan, whose eyes finally betrayed her, glistening in the reflection of the setting sun that streaked through the barred window behind Luna.

"Regan, if it were not for you, I would not have discovered a very significant link between the duke's family and my own. I only wish I'd have written down all I've experienced while away from you both. You would be walking in the fields behind our home for hours on end, delving into the pages of that diary," Luna said, eliciting a sad giggle from Regan.

Tobias lightly cleared his throat, signaling their time was drawing to a close. Luna swallowed, realizing her fate was resting on a village that had always been suspicious of her family, never fully accepting them. But the alternative was lifelong imprisonment, knowing Caedon was enduring the same – eternally with her, yet forever asunder.

In that moment, Luna truly grappled with which outcome she would rather have, but then quickly reminded herself it was out of her hands and tied into a destiny beyond her control.

"Dirdra, there is something I must tell you that my mother and father did not tell you because ... well, because they still had me," Luna said. "As you know, once my father died, the deed to our estate was passed down to my cousin on my father's side, Melvan, but in name, only — as he had included a request that I be in charge of running the household and property in Melvan's absence. Another stipulation my father made was that if something were to happen to me, Melvan was to do with the property as he saw fit. I have written him to tell him you are more than capable of running that household, if he should choose to keep it and lease the property. And if he should choose to sell it, he has agreed to take you and Regan on at his farmstead."

Dirdra began to shake her head, but saw her instinctual obstinacy would be useless. The decision had been made.

"There should be enough saved up to tide you both over for now, and well, Dirdra, you practically ran our home for most of the time my father was ill," Luna said, feeling a peculiar sense of peace in talking about the familiar.

Both Dirdra and Regan slowly nodded, sensing Tobias stirring impatiently behind them. Dirdra pulled Luna into a brisk embrace, barely able to contain her anguish as she whispered words of strength into Luna's ear. She brusquely turned away and walked to the door, never looking back.

Regan stood for a few seconds, her breathing beginning to pick up, creating a slight friction between them. Before Luna could say anything, Regan rushed forward and kissed her hard on the lips, sending waves of tortured elation jolting through Luna's veins.

But just as suddenly as she crashed into her, Regan ripped herself away, throwing one last grief-stricken glance at her before running into the shadows.

Luna brought her fingertips slowly to her lips, slightly ajar as she blankly stared at the spot Regan had just stood, in bewilderment. The depth of her friend's true emotions pierced Luna's heart.

The world turned fuzzy for a few moments, flooding her ears with deafening static. It was not until she felt herself being jostled by Tobias' stern hand that she remembered he was there.

Ripping her tearful eyes from that spot, Luna brought them to Tobias.

"Luna, are you able to comprehend what I am about to tell you?" he asked, his voice almost entirely devoid of emotion.

Luna felt her heart wring in response. She could only nod and swallow as a tear glanced down the side of her hand, still pressed against her lips.

"The village has reached a consensus."

Chapter 32

Luna's heart plummeted as she stared at Tobias' lips. They moved like molasses, each word carefully enunciated.

"Miss Fortella. The village has deliberated. I have met with the head of every household as decreed by King Bertrem," Tobias said. "The general consensus for the two charges of murder and sacrilege brought forth against you is ... punishment by death."

As though gravity doubled its pull, the grinding pebbles beneath her engulfed Luna. Tobias instinctively jerked forward, but was blocked by the bars, helpless to catch her. Instead, he regained himself and stood up, waiting for Luna to gather herself.

A few moments passed as she took several deep breaths. It was then she noticed the steady drip from a pipe in the cell next to her. It kept time with the raucous thud of her heartbeat. Slowly, she turned her face toward Tobias, concentrating on each exhale.

"Miss For– Luna," Tobias said, his voice softening upon her name. "I may have had authority to override it had it been a closer decision. But, it was, well, it was overwhelming, the support against you."

Luna had stopped listening, continuing to home in on the ceaseless trickle of that rusty pipe. It was only the last words he spoke that sliced through her haze.

"You have three days and one request ... within reason."

Luna's milky eyes, pale with defeat, bore into Tobias. Every ounce of emotion pulsing through her vocal cords betrayed her in the end, leaving her speechless. She clenched her jaw, feeling the violent ache in her chest expand, and continued to hold his gaze. There was only one thing Luna wanted, and he knew what it was.

Tobias started to shake his head, but gradually stopped, pursing his lips.

"I will see what I can do," he simply said, before pivoting sharply toward the doors, slamming them behind him.

*****

Held firmly in place by two sturdy prison guards, Caedon awaited the soft clank that accompanied the large, brass key being inserted into the prison door's iron lock. His heart skipped in tormented desperation as the lock shifted and the wooden doors were pulled open, filling his ears with a despondent melody wafting through the damp air.

It did not take Caedon long to realize the mournful, raspy notes came from her lips, sadness dripping from every syllable. A second set of doors appeared past the shadows of the hallway as the guards stiffly shoved Caedon forward. They were swiftly unlocked, and Caedon pushed through.

The song abruptly ended as Caedon's shackled legs moved toward the melody's lingering remnants, echoing through the metal bars. As he drew nearer, he made out her vague silhouette wearily standing in the warm light of the torches around her cell, squeezing his heart with trepidation.

His eyes caught hers, aflame with momentary life despite the cries of a merciless village crowd pulsing beyond her barred window. But none of that mattered to him. Luna was alive – tattered and nearly broken, but alive.

Caedon's eyes skimmed over her exquisite frame, taking in every scrape, bruise and lashing. Briefly overcome with ire, he squeezed his eyes shut before opening them to her violent pupils, emanating anguish over his own maimed state.

Both of their minds traveled to the last night they spent together, her soft limbs draped around his body as every inch of his skin was traced by her supple lips.

Unable to stand still any longer, Caedon rushed forward, bringing his tied hands to the bar before him, clasping her quivering fingers. The sudden movement triggered one of the guards to step forward, stayed only by the quick arm and sharp look of the second.

Caedon's energy charged Luna's deprived skin, sending waves of euphoria through her bones as his lips crashed into her mouth. Her tongue parted his lips, submerging them into silence. The stirring village, shifting guards, dripping pipe vanished before them, amplifying each trembling breath.

A gust of wind tore through the cell, building the flames as they danced on the walls around them, igniting their tears. The first guard cleared his throat, piercing the silence.

"It is time," he simply said, stepping forward and grasping Caedon's right upper arm. Caedon bit back the urge to unsheathe every ounce of rage that quivered beneath his skin. His brooding, storm-filled irises expanded as his pupils narrowed with each wave of anger pulsing through him. But then his eyes found her temples once more – so soft they had once felt beneath his lips – before he caught her pleading gaze.

Even now, facing death, she cared more for his life than her own. It was then he let reality truly sink in.

Nothing could be done. They both knew it.

"I love you," he whispered violently, his body pulled back by both guards, shattering his grip from her hands, her pulse.

"I love you," she managed through cracked vocal cords.

And just like that, he was gone.

*****

A crippling pool of despair eddied beneath her, creating an abysmal vacuum that enveloped her body, sending her rocking back and forth on her knees. She closed her eyes, summoning a picture of Caedon's face, his eyes the color of a robin's egg. Suddenly, his eyes crinkled around the edges, his entire face morphed into that of her father, eyes sparkling the way they would every time she entered the room. Burying her eyelids into the palms of her gritty hands, Luna let out several low moaning sobs, missing her father so much she could hardly breathe. The image in her mind further distorted to a pair of potent jade eyes framed by long, dark tendrils.

Her mother.

Luna slowly stopped rocking, though her eyes remained clamped, desperate to keep such a rare, lucid vision alive. She studied every line of her mother's face, her eyes sadly looking upon Luna as her head subtly nodded. It was as though her mother was answering the unspoken question in her daughter's eyes.

Is this my fate?

Yet, Cybele's eyes never wavered. They grew darker as Luna strived to hold her image just a few moments longer. The vertical crease between her mother's eyebrows deepened as Luna realized she was growing angry, stronger and yet serene all at the same time. Her mother's body shifted into an image of an oak tree with a burrow at the center and a beating heart split in two. The branches extended, showing ghostly flashes of various eyes tied to multiple soul energies running through each branch, like electric veins. The soul energies were all connected and pulsing, as though wanting to expand but entrapped by an unseen force. Their energy flowed toward the deep burrow. Luna stared at the heart in the center, her breath catching as she recognized the eye flashing on the left side as her own, and the eye glowing to right, as Caedon's.

Suddenly, within the tree's bark, Luna saw several images of her and Caedon come into form, then disappear. They did not look as they do now. Their bodies morphed and changed. Memories flooded Luna's mind at a pace she could hardly bear. She gasped as she felt centuries of life pour into her, feeling as though her brain would burst at the seams.

She saw various versions of herself – always hiding, controlled and abused, lifetime after lifetime. And Caedon always saved her. It was a loop. A loop they were caught in. Yet as Luna looked deeper into her own eyes, she saw the moon reflecting back at her, and the tips of flames burning and growing with each death and rebirth, with each dark, oppressive life experience she endured.

Her mind's eye landed on her most recent lifetime before this one. She saw herself held captive by two men. Her ancestors' books filled with herbal remedies, incantations, prayers and decades of wisdom had been confiscated and burned. Her body appeared tattered and bruised. As she stared into the eyes of the two men, she realized one of them was her husband. His eyes were dark and void of emotion. She gasped as she realized it was Darius. The other man was his brother. Her stomach twisted into knots as she recognized his sage eyes. Father Geirnuk.

She remembered being promised to Darius, a wealthy nobleman. She remembered hating everything about him. And then she recalled the moment she met a soldier. She remembered the way he looked at her – the recognition undeniable.

Caedon.

When Darius learned of their affair, he had searched her family's home, scouring every corner for evidence of more betrayals, but discovering her family's history in sorcery instead. He killed her parents and younger sister, whom Luna realized was Arianna. He planted evidence to frame Luna and tortured her before turning her over to the officials, where she was condemned for witchcraft and accused of killing her own family.

Luna felt intense rage building as each memory took hold. She watched, in horror, at what unfolded. In that lifetime, she hadn't been able to control her fear, her anger and her pain. She watched as her entire body began to boil from the inside. She saw her prison cell catching fire, then watched as flames licked the walls, spreading into the entire building. She saw Darius and his brother desperately scrambling to get outside as the fire burned the prison guards to ash. She watched as the fire spread along the ground, through a shallow line of trees, following the brothers as they ran toward the village. She gasped as she saw the flames threatening to take hold of her entire village. She remembered feeling a rage and desire for vengeance so deep, she could not control it.

She saw Darius and his brother turn to look back before reaching the edge of the village. Their eyes widened in horror as they watched Luna walking toward them slowly, subtle flickers of flames trailing behind her. She remembered focusing on their hearts, feeling heat building beneath their skin as their hands flew to their chests. She watched them die, slowly, painfully. Tears, like lava, flowed down her cheeks as she looked up at the sky, afraid of what would happen if she couldn't regain control.

"Luna, stop!"

Her breath caught as she heard his voice. She turned around and saw Caedon behind her, the soldier's hands raised, his blue eyes pleading. He approached her, unafraid, as though an innate part of him knew he had done this many times before. As he stepped within an inch of her, she felt the fire flickering in her eyes and smoldering inside of her begin to dissipate.

"Stop," he whispered, then wrapped his arms around her. Her body's heat – and the flames nearing the edge of the village – slowly dissolved, as villagers began to gather outside their homes, crying in fear and disbelief. Luna crumbled in Caedon's arms, sobbing.

Suddenly, Caedon swung both of their bodies around. She watched his eyes fly open as she heard the sound of a sword impale him from behind – Darius' attempt to kill Luna with his last breath, thwarted. Darius' eyes went placid as Caedon and Luna fell to the ground. She cradled his head in her arms, tears falling on his cheeks as she watched the life leave his beautiful eyes.

"You saved me," she cried.

"I will always save you," he whispered. She watched, in anguish, as he took his last breath.

Luna stood, staring at the villagers, their mouths agape, too afraid to move. She knew she had to flee or she would die. And then Caedon's sacrifice would have been in vain.

She ran, disappearing into the woods.

The vision began to dim in Luna's mind. The woods morphed back into the image of the oak tree.

Luna felt a momentary peace and resolve come over her as she stared at the stoically beautiful trunk and branches. And as her heartbeat grew steadier, the entire tree melted into an image of Luna's face.

Something shifted inside her. Yet now its movement felt familiar. She realized what her mother's eyes had been saying. This was her destiny. She knew what she must do to finally break the cycle of lifetimes past – what she and Caedon must learn to fulfill their karma, to fulfill the karmas of their soul tribe, to free them all. While her human mind could not understand why they were chosen for this role, her soul knew the path to its destiny the moment it crossed paths with Caedon's. He would not make the ultimate sacrifice this time. He would not be her savior this time.

She would be his.

She would be all of theirs.

Luna stared at her mirrored self a few moments more, watching her eyes grow darker before the image dissipated, bringing her back to her current reality.

She fluttered her eyes open to the rowdy cries of villagers outside her cell, signaling Caedon's presence. She heard the stubborn clank of her cell door opening as a guard stepped in and bent down to retrieve her. Luna's eyes shot up at him, flames swirling beneath her pupils.

He straightened and took a small step back, apprehensively allowing her room to rise on her own. Wincing as her aching feet bore her weight once more, Luna shakily stood and took a step past the guard as he followed at her heels.

Her skin mimicked the flames of the torches around her, smoldering beneath her withered peasant skirt and blouse. The guard, feeling the strange heat trailing behind her, kept a bit more distance between himself and her back as she walked down the mold-infested hallway and through the large prison doors.

Smoke-filled dusk air assailed Luna's senses as a throng of people ruptured into shrieks and howls. She stood there a moment, taking in the village beyond the crowd, barely catching a glimpse of her manor. She wondered whether Dirdra and Regan were there now. She knew they were not here. She felt it in the deepest regions of her heart.

Poor Regan.

Luna let out a temperate breath, giving her head a slight shake. The dark tresses that had fallen from her mother's scarf framed her face as she took a moment to wipe her eyelids with her bound wrists.

Then, channeling the grace of her mother, Luna stepped forward.

With each step she took, the horde of villagers began to divide, creating a path to the wooden steps several feet ahead. This time, Luna's eyes never touched the ground. She looked straight ahead as she ambled her way through the crowd, feeling a mixture of scathing, fearful and compassionate looks graze the edges of her awareness.

Words of malice and mercy billowed around her, but her mind, heart and soul were elsewhere. They were desperately searching for another's.

His face, buried by the four, armed guards surrounding him, stretched upward to catch a glimpse of her. He had been forced to watch. But Caedon knew, deep down, there would never have been a choice.

His dismal eyes found Luna's as he watched them transform, momentarily overcome by ethereal silvery hues. But just as quickly, they clouded over when the guard behind her urged her up the steps, her lithe form practically floating to the platform before them.

Suddenly, silence cloaked them both, betraying only the acute thrum of their heartbeats as the guard untied her wrists and ripped them backward to bind them around the wooden pole biting at her back.

She winced ever so slightly, causing snickers in the crowd and a low growl from Caedon as he clenched his jaw. However, her eyes never broke from his, her lips still swollen from his kiss.

Smoke swirled around her body as surrounding flames licked her skin, igniting her ashen eyes, which appeared sable in the shadows of the blaze. Mouths dropped, eliciting gasps from the crowd. A dark figure near the bottom of the steps stirred, shifting everyone's attention to his form.

"Any last words?" Father Geirnuk asked, his callous voice oozing feigned rectitude.

Luna never blinked, her gaze locked on Caedon's cobalt irises ... the reflection of her soul. Her twin flame.

This is real.

Everything else is an illusion.

Caedon started forward, emotion bleeding from his eyes, but the guards jerked him firmly back in place.

She shook her head sadly, the brimming tear in her left eye finally diving down her cheek, searing her skin. The priest droned on, something about her wicked soul and God's mercy. She listened to none of it.

Every emotion surfaced then, playing across her eyes. Anger boiled, swirling like a whirlpool of black lava, smoldering any ray of hope left. Its wickedness – a wave of intense heat that ripped through the crowd – caused several people to step back as even Caedon's eyes widened.

But as the flames began to swallow her, she grew slack, forcing her vengeful mind to make way for her heart. And in its magnificence, the abysmal emotion of her heart poured out of her and streamed into Caedon, stealing his breath.

"Luna" he sputtered, collapsing into the stoic grips of the guards.

His eyes shut, squeezing tears beneath them and closing out her image and the piercing screams around him. She followed suit, exhaling as she clamped down her eyelids, shutting out the scalding blaze around her, its smoke clawing at her lungs.

She heard nothing but the ocean, smelling only the scent of his skin.

He invoked the image of her angelic body in his mind, splayed out next to his only a few nights prior. Moonbeams had blanketed her feathery skin as they glistened in his eyes.

She looked up at him through her lashes sadly.

You cannot save me this time, my love.

He shook his head in anguish, looking into her beautiful eyes.

The crowd grew uneasy, as her pupils began to narrow and her eyes became dark and stormy.

Flames appeared at the center of her irises as her hair swept up in a violent frenzy around her porcelain skin and dark lips.

I must save you.

Epilogue

King Bertrem stared at the chicken stew quickly cooling in front of him. It was his favorite entrée, yet he could not bring himself to touch it, his appetite lost along with his spirits. He subconsciously shook his head, still baffled by his reaction to the recent transgressions within his realm.

He could not wrap his mind around why this all felt different from any other trials, executions and condemnations he had carried out in his many years of reign, including his own brother's betrayal. Yet, in some way, his heart and soul were unsettled by the fate that befell his trusted confidant, Duke Nicolai, and his sons, Caedon and Darius. But even more so, the servant girl.

Luna.

He quickly buried the image of her into the back of his mind ... into the darkest corners of his consciousness.

The king wearily peered out the stained glass window to his right, seeing the cloudy skies for the first time that day. They seemed to brood and churn with foreboding. He let out a lengthy exhale, feeling his lungs depress beneath his ribcage.

Suddenly, his chamber doors flew open as two guards stumbled in. King Bertrem's eyes, wide with momentary shock, quickly narrowed at the unkempt appearance of the men who haphazardly bowed before him.

"What is the meaning of this?" he demanded, abruptly standing and cursing as his hip banged into the table, causing his stew to spill over.

The guards quickly composed themselves, realizing their disgraceful actions, and bent their heads lower.

"We apologize, Your Majesty," said the guard closest to the king, staring at the carpet below him.

"You may rise," the king said, pulling on his tunic before sitting back down in his chair, his stew long forgotten.

"Your Excellency, please excuse our intrusion, but we have come to inform you of a most troubling discovery," the guard continued, now meeting the king's eyes, which hardened at his words.

"What troubling discovery?" King Bertrem asked, his teeth beginning to grind.

"There has been a breach in prison security. That is the only explanation," the second guard sputtered.

"The only explanation for what?" the king asked, his patience wearing dangerously thin.

"The only explanation, Your Highness, for the apparent escape of a prisoner," the first guard quickly inserted.

King Bertrem's hands clenched into fists on the tabletop as he leaned forward, his eyes drilling into the guard's face.

"Which prisoner?" he said, his tone eerily forbearing.

"The banished duke's son, your Grace, ... Caedon."

The king jolted from the table and was in front of the guards in a flash, causing them to cower.

"Take me to his cell right now," he commanded.

The startled guards scrambled to their feet and led the king to the prison. As King Bertrem approached Caedon's vacant cell, he felt a strange energy crackling near his temples. He chose to ignore it as he rounded the corner and came face to face with the empty barred room. As he squinted into the dimly lit chamber, he noticed something black on the floor.

"What is that?" he said, pointing to the object. One of the guards stepped inside the cell and retrieved the item, holding it out to the king.

"Your Majesty," he simply said as the king grabbed hold of it, bringing it under the candlelight.

It was a black lace scarf.

As though moved by a force unknown to him, the king instantly brought the cloth to his nose, inhaling. The guard cleared his throat in response, nervously glancing away. After a few moments, the king's eyes suddenly widened.

"I must go to my stables," he announced, briskly pivoting on his left foot and hurriedly walking up the staircase.

Moments later, King Bertrem stood in front of his stable doors, fervently waiting for one of his guards to bring the key. He noticed his breath crystallize in the cool air as he finally heard the lock shift and the door open.

Every stride felt like an eternity as the king approached the second-to-last stall on his right. He heard the movement of hooves against straw, though he could not be sure which stall they came from. His eyes briefly flitted to the nameplate.

Libra.

He grabbed the brass handle and pulled it toward him, hearing its creaks groan beneath its weight as the earthy scent of hay and oats arrested his senses. Momentarily overcome, the king closed his eyes as the door swung past him. When he finally snapped them open, he heard the guards' gasps.

The stall was empty.

The king's eyes darted to the floor, frantically following Libra's hoof prints, which led to the rear stable entrance. The guards ambled behind him as he reached the large oak doors and yanked them open.

When he looked down again, past the stable threshold, his breath caught in the mist.

The prints were gone.

The End.

About the Author

Cassandra is a Cleveland, Ohio-based author whose writing is influenced by her passion for the mystical arts, her Romanian heritage and strong female archetypes.

Professionally, she also serves as the editor of three local newspapers, teaches yoga, practices as a Reiki Master and an intuitive, and avidly seeks knowledge in the holistic arts realm. When she's not spending time with her spoiled cat, Bella, she loves writing poetry and short stories, reading, sketching, traveling, learning, and playing piano and guitar.

Made in the USA
Monee, IL
05 June 2020